Agents 1

Agents 1

We're a Team, Deal with It!

Anushka Arvind

PARTRIDGE
A Penguin Random House Company

ISBN: Softcover   978-1-4828-5991-1
             eBook   978-1-4828-5990-4

To order additional copies of this book, contact
Partridge India
000 800 10062 62
orders.india@partridgepublishing.com

www.partridgepublishing.com/india

Contents

Acknowledgements

I would like to thank my parents, friends and relatives for their support in the writing of this book. This book is based on my imagination and it's meant for the enjoyment of all readers. It is the first of a series of three.

This is to the friends who always aided me with my stories and give their opinion on them. It helped me a lot, especially in this book. Also to all those who still pass comments on seeing me scribbling stuff.

My parents supported me very much in writing stories and always answered any queries related to what I wanted to know. This book series is not connected to my previous book though some things might be coincident. I would like to thank those who helped me in getting details right of this book, i.e., internet, maps, people etc.

Whatever situation this book portrays, whether good or bad, is just a situation. I respect all types of people, culture, etc., equally.

I also thank my publisher for their help.

This series portrays a sense of a story which can be real if you, the reader, believes in it. It is based on my perspective of certain things and I hope you will like a young writer's work. At last, I humbly thank you. Enjoy!

Dedications

To my best friends...

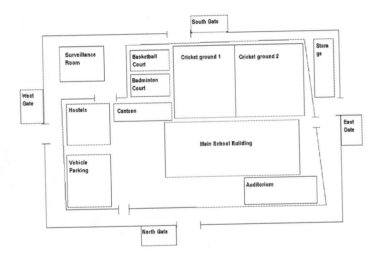

Chapter One – New School?!

On just a regular day, in the outskirts of the west side of the bustling city of Hyderabad there was National Highway 202, with the coming and going of vehicles. One side of the road had a few agricultural fields and in the distance beyond were a few hills to be seen with a forest underneath.

This was a cover, of course.

Suddenly, a female figure on a hover board appeared out of the forest and she was chased by a bunch of other male figures on hover boards! As she tried to get away, they were on her tail, edging closer to her! The male figures started shooting and the female figure kept dodging their bullets like a professional!

She went over a hill and through a tunnel but they were still behind her! She increased her speed and was about to crash into a hill when suddenly, she takes a sharp turn and a few figures crashed instead!

You won't get me that easily!

But there were still more behind her! Again she increased her speed, went towards another mountain and did the same by taking another sharp turn with the rest of them crashing into it. The female figure pops out safely behind the hill and sees all of the crashed figures.

I told you! Ha!

She headed towards the bunch of hills and in the valley below there was the IB special training base. She took a descent slowly at the common helipad, located behind a hill of the 5 acre government centre. This place was camouflaged in the most possible professional way ever, courtesy of the army.

She took off her helmet with one hand showing her medium length of wavy long black hair tied in a braid, and her sunglasses with another, showing her dark brown eyes. She folded the glasses, got down from her hover board and turned it off. Then she took off her military green jacket showing a black full sleeved jersey having the white IB logo on it. She was tanned and very fit.

Anyway, this was a test given by the high officials of the IB for young recruits to be selected in the top 400 and the top 50 team of agents throughout the country. The official in charge of this army base was an army officer working under the LSS. He was present as their examiner and he observed her every move. She goes to him and they shook hands.

"Let's see... Agent Khanna...", he said, as he was noting down stuff in his clipboard.

"Yes, sir?" she replied.

"I've heard of your father. Amazing guy!" he said.

Usually candidates are tested in four aspects: Shooting, combat, intelligence and agility. These four have equal weight age. All test scores clubbed define the post of the candidate.

The female figure was Candidate Simran Khanna who was in the top agent training base. She is caring, friendly but a serious and a really straightforward girl. She gets temper mental for the right reasons but controls her attitude in front of others. She's very observant that makes her intelligent.

"Agility test...is this the final one?" he asked.

"Yes sir!" she said.

"You scored well. Compiling all test scores your final score is 50 out of 50. You are hereby one of the top 400 and top 50 agents of the IB".

I topped?

"Thank You, sir!"

"I've heard that you have been working very hard for the position. Congratulations. You've got into my good graces."

"Thank you very much! I did work hard! Thank you!"

"Would you like to see your family first or leave for the place where you'll be assigned?"

"I'll leave for the assigned place!"

"Well, go back to your cabin and await my orders on where you are assigned. We don't know when you'll leave so pack your bags quickly".

"Yes, sir!" she said and turned to go but stopped and turned around.

"Sorry but I have a question! Sir!" she said.

"Ask quickly! I don't have much time!" he said.

"How come two people here are selected for the top 50 when it's supposed to be only one?" she asked.

"You and the other agent passed. And since the Bangalore army base had no standard for their top 50, Agent Chopra will go as well! Now leave and await your orders!" he said.

"Yes, sir! Thank you, sir!" she said.

"You don't need to thank me!" he said.

"Sorry was I not supposed to?" she asked.

What's wrong in saying that?

"Just leave and await your orders, Agent Khanna!" he said.

She left in a puzzled way to her cabin.

Her cabin was a concrete five-storied building covered (camouflaged) in the colours of the hills. Simran goes to the cabin and climbs up the stairs to the second floor turning into the first door on her right where she finds Candidate Radhika Chopra (her roommate), who has also passed her final test and is awaiting orders. She is best in combat, intelligence and agility. But shooting wasn't working out for her.

Black shoulder length curly hair, glasses and very skinny with a creamy skin tone(unlike Simran's light brown tan) but tough as she won her district and state boxing tournaments twice.

She is damn short tempered but always calms down and solves a problem with a plan. She is also a nerd and a bit lazy too.

Radhika was packing her bag when she saw her and gave her a hug. Simran goes and sits down on a chair in a very tired way.

"We just finished the test, why are you ready?" asked Simran, seeing her dressed up wearing a fitting black t-shirt, tight blue jeans with sneakers on.

"We have to leave after a while. You'd better get ready too. How was the test?" asked Radhika.

"I topped, actually..." Simran replied.

"Nobody does. Is it above 45?" asked Radhika.

"50 on 50. You?" she asked.

"46!" she replied.

"Radhika, just think! We are going to be two of the Top 50!" said Simran, while grabbing a towel and wiping herself.

"You are. You scored more!"

"No, we both are!"

"How? Only one person per base!"

"No agent passed the test from the Bangalore base so we both are selected! And we both are together!"

"We trained for so long!"

"I know! You've been there since we were 5."

"So were you! But really though, how are you so sure? What if we're in different stations?"

"I took a peak at the examiner's mark sheet. That's the only explanation! I wonder which LOCKER will we be at!"

At that time the entered saying "Attention top 50 agents! Since you both scored well in your teamwork tests, you both are going to the same place. It's the most important. Rohtang Residential School. You will complete your class 11 and 12, take care of LOCKER 01."

"Where is that?" asked Radhika.

"Assam." He said.

"So far? Where do we stay?" asked Simran.

"It's a residential school." Said the. "A very big and important one at that.

I didn't expect the most important one for us!

"Yes school… and I see that your bags have been packed. You will board a flight to Guwahati airport and from that station your train will go to Duar junction. I will have someone waiting there for you both! Understood?" said the.

"Yes, sir!" said the two of them.

He hands them their tickets and leaves.

"Again we have to change our school..." muttered Simran.

"I didn't enjoy the last one anyway!" says Radhika.

"Everybody would tease you because of your glasses, that's it! And I do admit, that frame made you look like a cat!"

"I don't wear them much anymore and I changed my frame! Please leave the topic or else..."

"Fine! I left it!"

"Anyway, why didn't you go home? Don't tell me that-"

"What about you?"

"They are at a funeral of a relative. They advised me not to go! But what about-"

"Just don't ask!"

"Okay fine! Anyway, let's go! We'll be late!"

"Right!"

After packing, they went out with their bags and loaded them into the trunk of a car. They noticed everybody not selected leaving the base with their bags.

The rest of the agents, a few selected, in the top 400 entered a jeep in military uniform behind them, while giving envious looks. Radhika noticed a boy getting in and they had a moment of eye contact. She immediately tugged Simran's shoulder disturbing her reading her tablet.

"Simran! See him! He's the guy who was looking at me all the time! Come on! See once!" she said.

"No, it doesn't matter. You are getting worked up. And I'm not interested in seeing him!" she said without lifting her head up from her tablet.

"It's really important! He's very weird! Just look up for a second!" – the boy goes to the back and sat down with his back facing them – "Damn! You missed him again!" she said, pissed off.

"There's a reason why I don't see! It's because I have better things to do other than checking out boys like you!" she said again not lifting her head up.

Damn her...what's the issue in seeing?!

They sat in the car with the official sitting in front of them with the driver. As they reached the highway, the official explained a few things.

"Listen to me carefully. Taking care of LOCKER 01 is not easy at all. First, the in charge/Principal is the most strict. Obey her. Next, be careful when the Border Security Force soldiers or IB officials come and inspect how you work. The last thing, always carry your devices issued to you in the rule book." – the car stopped and her opened the door – "Agent Khanna, we expect great things from you. All the best at your new school." He said, got out and closed the door of the car then left.

From me?!

They reached the Hyderabad airport. They both got out of the car and went inside. The agents then separated themselves to go to different boarding gates. The two top 50 agents reached their boarding gate and were on time. They checked in their tickets and baggage then boarded their plane. Within three hours the plane made a swatch at the Kolkata airport then it flew straight to the Guwahati airport in one hour. From there they went in a taxi to the train station and got in a train on platform number 8. After a couple of hours, they reached the Duar junction. They get down with their bags on platform number 2 and head out of the station.

"Will we be able to identify her?" asked Radhika after they put their bags down and sat down on a bench just outside the station.

"Her name is Indira. Agent Indira Jaiswal! She's a local here!" says Simran while showing a photograph of her.

"Which base did she pass out from?" asked Radhika, while looking at the picture.

"The army base in Shillong. She's been a student in this school for 4 years!" said Simran.

"You already read up on her!" said Radhika.

"That's what I was doing all this time. I tried finding out as much as I could other than this information. We should, you know!" said Simran.

"Yeah...mind telling me stuff about them too?" asked Radhika."Knowledge is to be shared, you know!"

"Sure it is...when you didn't read up!" said Simran.

"You think she's friendly?" asked Radhika.

"I've never seen any agent friendly!" said Simran.

"Not everybody should be like you!" said Radhika.

"Shut up, I'm all right!" she said.

They waited for some time and noticed a girl with long… long hair tied into a braid, wearing a shirt and jeans and having a cute fair face emerge from the crowd and head towards them. She's short but has enough strength to take on anybody.

"Hi! You must be Radhika Chopra and Simran Khanna. Come on! We haven't got all day! I'm Indira but you can just call me Indu! I was here for a while, a couple weeks ago. Many of us were. Also just like you, I'll be staying in the hostels too. Actually we agents have to. And even I'm one of the Top 50 class teenage agents of the IB!" said Indira. Indira Jaiswal is damn talkative. Most of the stuff she says is a bit stupid or useless. She's friendly too and very kind. She also elaborates on things too much. Her test score was 45 out of 50. She's best in combat, agility and a little shooting.

Wow, she's really friendly!

Simran and Radhika stared at her.

"Umm… okay I think I've got it!" says Radhika.

"Did anyone tell that you talk too much?" says Simran.

"I get that a lot! Sorry I can't help it! Anyway let's go! There's the school car! Hand over your bags to the driver!" says Indira.

"It's fine. I'll handle my bags myself!" said Simran and helped the driver put their bags in the trunk.

"Thanks for the help!" said the driver.

"Sure! You too!" said Simran.

When Simran and the driver were done loading they got into the car and set off.

In the car,

"So! Enough of me! Tell me something about you both!" said Indira.

"We've just passed out of the LSS training camp at Hyderabad!" said Radhika.

"Okay…" says Indira, expecting more description.

"And that's it!" said Radhika.

"That's it? Damn, you guys talk so less! Seriously, you should be happy about the decision they made! You made history in the IB!" said Indira.

Huh?

It was a policy of the agency to round up equal amount of top 50 agents from different training centres at major cities, not only state capitals. One from each are always selected but it was a first that two were selected by one training centre for the top 50.

They both were sceptically looking at her.

"Oh, too bad! Our habit and thanks for the compliment!" said Radhika, sarcastically.

"So, what do we have to do here?" asks Simran, changing the topic.

"This school has the most important LOCKER in the country and it needs more familiar security. Basically the fellow agents you meet here are the toppers of the recruitment test. All of them. Some are also not to be messed with too. I'm just cautioning you but bottom line, we need to maintain security and also patrol the perimeter. We only get to apprehend those who wish to get their hands on the LOCKER. Got it?" explains Indira.

"Rohtang Residential School" is situated 75 kilometres away from the banks of the river Brahmaputra at the border of India and Bhutan in Assam. The nearest town or village is only 20 kilometres away from the school and the nearest army base is 50 kilometres away. The school is a 15 acre campus with four gates which are north, south, east and west. The students of the school come from a train station which is at least 40 kilometres away from the school as well. There is security necessary in it because one of the vaults under the LSS is located there. It stores sealed files of the government that are not to be accessed by anybody. Nobody except high post IB officials know where they are and the security should be influenced dutiful agents who don't ask questions about them. So the Intelligence Bureau (IB) created a program called the Locker Security Squad (LSS) to select teenagers as security for protecting the LOCKERs. Their function is only to protect the LOCKER, not the students(unless a few are assigned to protect any particular person residing in the school only when an authorised official orders to do so).

"Yeah, got it!" says both of them.

"Also, listen! The timings are the same every day. School timings are 8:50am to 3:00pm. At our patrol areas we shouldn't go during school hours. Only if the Princi calls us for meetings in our hidden meeting room near the LOCKER, then only we go. Our patrol timings are from 5:30 to 9:00pm. You have to meet the Princi after you unpack at the hostels to know where you'll patrol. Also, on Sunday, patrolling is from 1:00 to 9:00pm. Got it?" she asked.

"Sure! Uh, no I-" Radhika started.

"It's okay! I've got it!" said Simran.

The first LSS was established in 1978 after the burning of crucial files by a top minister during the final period of the state of emergency declared nationwide. The IB created vaults called Lockers and distributed them around the country in remote areas. All over the country there are 30LOCKERs(5 big LOCKERs are located in border schools and the rest are in places with a few villages) and for the security of them, they are stored under schools and offices which aren't that known to most people. Only few locals and a few high post IB officials know about the existence of these. Security were adult agents but they proved to be a problem due to the suspicions of the people working normally there. After a major robbery by a wanted agent on one such LOCKER in 1983, the IB started to recruit youngsters and established an elite top 400 armed undercover agent group which are scattered all over India as a few in every place of the LOCKER. But there was a problem of the top 400 and that was their education. So in 1985, the IB committee of young recruits decided to transfer the LOCKERs under offices only to schools so that those youngsters go to school and maintain security of the LOCKER while staying undercover. Every two years the top 400 change and a test is given by the bases in which at least a few from each base will get selected. One from each base is selected for the top 50. The top 50 was established in 1990 and was made because the agency had selective missions regarding the capture of criminals that were connected with the LOCKERs. This school was near the border and it had the most important LOCKER so there were more agents required.

"But won't the kids hate the job? It may be too much for them. They are just 16 to 17 years old!" said an official, objecting to the board of the IB when they took the decision that time.

"They are doing it for the country, for the priceless things not to be exposed at any cost. They will protect the nation's secrets!" said the Director at that time.

"What if they want to know?" the official asked again.

"They won't. They are kids who can be taken care of! And we will pass a bill to prevent anybody from knowing it. Not even an RTI can be filed. Stop objecting to the best decision we've made!" said a board member, getting annoyed.

(RTI –Right to Information Act.)

"I'm merely enquiring, it's my job to! You even gave them licenses to injure. What if they start killing?! It's highly dangerous!" he said.

"It's not, they are kids! If anything happens then we will take action!" said another member.

"Understand the fact that we cannot let any more files get destroyed because of our carelessness. Plus, they are teenagers. We will make them realize that this job is a service to the nation and that they should be ready to sacrifice anything for the protection of those files." Said the Director.

"Look, just promise to put them in posts of in any department of defence so they stay loyal! Please!" said the official.

"Oh, you just-" started a board member but the Director raised his hand to stop him.

"Don't raise your voice to one of the national advisors. He has a point and I give you assurance that this program will be known to very less people and to the top 400 we will guarantee posts for them in any defence department. That's final!" said the Director, giving his word.

Indira hands them a bunch of photos and explains "Also just a bit of information. A few years ago, these spies were caught and handed over to the IB. They have totally trained them and now they are a part of us! This year's recruits."

"We know that!" said Simran while looking through the photos.

"Some of them may be a bit mentally disturbed and it is also our duty to take care of them a bit if it happens! I'm informing you this even if you know because we have quite a few here." said Indira.

"Understood..." said Radhika.

These specific criminals were also very young. Whether they did petty crimes or professional ones, they were picked up, arrested, etc., and sent to either their families or foster homes. From there, if they were interested then they would join the bases of the top 400 taking a contract that they would submit themselves to the IB. The process of enrolling wasn't easy. There were no posters and advertisements about it. Only through connections there were enrolments. Most of the candidates were from foster homes.

Candidates from the top 400 make it to the top 50 from the bases. It was all through that one test at the end of two months of training. The passing mark for top 400 is 32 out of 50 and for top 50 was 44 out of 50. To qualify for top 400 an agent should be great in at least two parameters and for top 50 three parameters.

Sometimes, the ex criminals may still have their enemies after them and some get caught in a mental breakdown.

"So...if there are a few in this school, then they are good, huh!" said Simran.

"Of course!" said Indira. "One of them is in the top 50 too! I will tell who is later because you shouldn't mess with him!"

"Why? Does he annoy?" asked Simran.

"He has a problem with girls and has a huge temperament!" replied Indira.

"Oh, that's worse!" said Simran.

"So how many agents are there in the school?" asked Radhika.

"Well, there are at least sixteen which includes you both. And later two more agents are coming during the term." said Indira.

"So I'm in the MPC stream. What about you two?" she asked.

"BiPC!" they both replied.

They then reached the school. The car drove into the parking and stopped but Indira told the driver to go left towards the hostels. The car then stopped in front of the hostel gate and they got down with their stuff. While walking towards the girl's hostel, they saw a group of guys in the parking lot who were leaning on bikes and talking. The boy (dark black hair styled and fair, wearing a loose red t-shirt with a sleeveless jacket and blue jeans.) and the same height as her in the middle on a Yamaha caught Simran's eye. Looked a bit buff and agile.

Chapter Two – Night Duty.

"Who is he?" wonders Simran.

She looks inside the bunch of photos and finds his picture.

"*Arjun Singh...* Indu, who is he?" asks Simran.

"Oh! He's Agent Singh. A few years ago he was taken in by the IB. He is part of the top 50." explained Indira.

Arjun Singh is a proud, young fellow who hates girls and never respects others. He hates change. He always wants to do things by himself. He is so short tempered, and he never listens to anybody. He got 49 out of 50 in his test which was the highest in his base. Not much impressive in shooting but is better than most people in one thing which we will get to know later.

"Is he the one having a problem with girls?" asked Simran.

"It's how he is! He can just never accept the fact that a girl can do better than him!" said Indira.

"How come?" asked Simran.

"You'll get to know later! But sadly, none of the girls can beat him. He's the best in sports and he's clever." said Indira.

"How did you guess?"

"Out of all those guys, whom I'm assuming are the ones to work with for the next two years, he was the only one who wasn't checking out a girl!" said Simran.

"Oh, you got a good eye!" said Indira.

"Which base?" Radhika asked.

"Chandigarh." Replied Simran.

"Right...he is BiPC, though!" said Indira.

Simran sees him and Arjun notices her. They look at each other for a moment then Simran looked away.

"Hey! What are you doing?" asked Indira when she noticed.

"Nothing, he just looked at me!" replied Simran.

"Okay...but we should stay away from them!" interrupted Radhika.

"What's making you say that?" said Simran.

"Just check out the guy next to Arjun!"

"Just this once!"

They both see a guy leaning on a Honda bike with black hair and a bit of a plain tanned complexion with wearing a tight V-neck black sweater and dark blue jeans. A bit thin but strong.

"Clearly!" says Simran.

"That's Agent Raghav Patel! He's MPC! I'm sure he's your type!" piped Indira.

"Don't worry! He seems stupid." Whispered Simran to Radhika.

"How can you tell?" she asked.

"Just now, he leaned in such a way to show off that his bike tilted and he fell." Said Simran.

"Ahaa...you are getting better at noticing things!" said Radhika.

"My pleasure..." she replied.

Raghav Patel flirts a lot and he's one of the most intelligent agents even though his score was 45. A little stupid yet every girl falls for his tricks. He's helpful and nice to all. He's not good in shooting and intelligence but he's in the top 50 due to his high scores in the other two parameters.

"Hey, he's from the Delhi base!" said Indira.

"Shut Up!" says Radhika.

"Oh…ok! Let's go now!" says Indira, looking in their direction.

"What?" said both of them.

"Nothing!" lies Indira.

Both of them see whom she's looking at. It was a guy on Raghav's left with black hair and was also a bit tanned but more than Raghav and has a slight moustache wearing a loose black t-shirt and blue tracks. Looked fit and agile.

"Can we please just go?" begs Indira. "That's Agent Aakash Dey, best to stay away from him! Long story! He's been here for 4 years too!"

"A local as well…from Kohima!" Simran whispered to Radhika.

"Wait! How can you tell if he is a local?" asked Radhika.

"He is used to the weather here. You can see that t-shirt is so thin and loose to let cold air pass through!" she replied.

Aakash Dey is an angry person but also is charming(rarely). He's also good at athletics mostly, a bit good in combat and he's a bit clever. Also he loves to hate Indira and she vice versa. His test score is 45.

"Is he MPC too?" asked Simran.

"Yes, now let's go." She insisted.

"Ok, fine!" they both said.

They went through the hostel gates. The hostel was two tall buildings(each of six floors) joined together with a common ground floor having the gym at one end and a couple of rooms on each side with TVs in them. The left building was the Girls' hostel at the edge of the inner wall and the right building was the boys' hostel overlooking the canteen. The three of them reached thehostels and go to the main notice board in the ground floor to check the list of the room arrangements.

Fifth floor:

Room 1 – Priya Desai, NOT YET ASSIGNED. (class 11)

Room 2 – Natasha Rai, Aparna Deshpande. (class 11)

Room 3 – Indira Jaiswal, NOT YET ASSIGNED. (class 11)

Room 4 - Radhika Chopra, Aanya Kaur. (class 11)

Room 5 - Simran Khanna, Shreya Fernandez. (class 11)

"Lucky you two! Agent Fernandez is nice! Very good. But not that high for top 50." said Indira.

"Hmm..." Simran replied.

"She's tough and strong. It was also rumoured that she was associated with a criminal. I hope you understand what I mean by the word 'associated'!" Said Indira, very softly.

"What about my roommate?" asked Radhika.

"Agent Kaur barely passed. I don't even know what she's good at. Many of the girls beat her down because she was weak. She is MEC. Anyway, let's go! You have to meet Princi after unpacking!"

"Simran, where is Kaur from?" asked Radhika.

"She's from Delhi but she came from the Ranchi base due to that one getting full. Same case as us!" said Simran.

They go to their respective rooms and unpack. Aanya was not in the room but Shreya was. She had really short black hair, brown eyes with a couple of spots on her face, about 5 feet 5 inches like Simran and was dark brown skinned. Very muscular.

Simran was impressed at her doing push ups down next to her bed while counting.

"98...99...100! Ah! Enough for today! New student?" asked Shreya while getting up on a chair, adjusting her blue t-shirt and white shorts and relaxing with a bottle of water.

Simran put her bag on her bed and unpacked. Shreya closed the door with the curtains while she noticed Simran's gun and bullets with a good laptop and tablet on her bed as she took them out and kept them.

Shreya Fernandez has a lot of attitude but that's only for display. She finds a way out of everything. The fittest girl ever seen. Unfortunately not top 50, her test score is 42.

"Yeah I'm Simran, are you Shreya?" asked Simran.

"Yeah. Hi!" she said, while taking a gulp of water from her bottle.

"Hey!" said Simran.

"Cute collection! I have a few too, yet yours look better!" she said, noticing the number of guns on the bed.

"I rarely use them. It doesn't matter if the gun's better, it depends on the shooter." Said Simran.

"No wonder. I'm not much of a shooter. I passed with my agility and combat!" said Shreya.

"What do you plan on doing later? Navy?" asked Simran, noticing Shreya's laptop open with the website of the Indian army.

"Yeah, you saw, huh. I'm MPC, though." She said.

She's from Panaji! Hmm...the best in those parameters are always from there.

Simran and Radhika left to the Principal's office with Indira. When they were ushered in, they stood in front of her. Simran was surprised a bit. The Principal, Agent Vijayanti Rao, is a strict official who did understand the agents. She is also undercover with them and she has a higher post at the

IB. She has tanned skin, glasses and a light green saari on. She was signing various documents when they had come in.

"Agent Simran Khanna and Agent Radhika Chopra! Right?" confirmed the Principal, looking up once at them.

"Yes, ma'am!" they replied.

"Good to see you, Agent Khanna. Agent Jaiswal, did you explain the timings?" asked the Principal.

"Oh, I forgot one thing! Every patrol area will have a girl and a boy there. So you should not have any objection with it!" said Indira.

"No, we don't!" said Simran.

"Anyway, I am busy at the moment so just grab those two papers and the small bags there and go to duty tomorrow night. Those bags are important and there are badges in them for your missions when you encounter other defence officials. Do not lose them. The ones you will be partnered up with will tell you what to do! Understood?" said the Principal.

"Yes, ma'am!" they said.

Each top 50 agent is issued a badge and no matter where they went, they have to take their badge along with them. The bags contained various devices or gadgets to help them in their job.

They took their papers and left with Indira. In the corridor, they check out their places at duty.

"You know her?" asked Radhika.

"She's a friend of my father." Replied Simran.

"That's pretty cool, Simran! Anyway, check your patrol areas!" said Indira.

"East gate?" said Radhika, after opening her paper.

"Oh, awesome!" said Indira.

"Why is it awesome?" she asked.

"Oh, you'll see! Another top 50 agent is there!" said Indira.

"Simran, what about yours?"

"Oh, nothing!" she said.

"Come on! Tell!" said Radhika.

"Oh, you'll see!" she said.

"By the way, Indu! Are you also a top 50 agent?" asked Radhika.

"Yes, I am! I will introduce everybody as soon as possible." said Indira. "Also, if you need anything then ask me anytime!"

"Okay..." they both replied.

"Also, sorry again! I forgot one last thing! For the 11th and 12th class students, classes finish by lunch. After lunch, science stream students have coaching classes till 4:00pm then leave. We agents don't have these classes. Instead, at this time, we have to complete home works, assignments, projects, etc., then leave." Said Indira.

"Oh!" said Simran.

"Got it!" said Radhika.

In the evening, the dinner bell strikes. Everyone started going to the canteen, started grabbing their plates and started occupying tables. Simran arrives late and sees the entire place already filled up.

Damn! All full!

She keeps looking around and could only see a place near Arjun.

Hostel room or here? Fine! How bad should he be?

She goes towards the table and sits down.

Arjun looked up at her.

"Mind if I sit here?" Simran asked.

"Nope."

"Thanks!"

She sat down opposite to Arjun and started eating while he was still noticing her. Just then, she looked up and he looked down at his plate.

"What?" she asked.

"Nothing, you were with Indu, right?" he said.

"Yeah! She picked us up from the station." she said.

This guy eats a lot…

"She talks a lot. But welcome to the top 400!" he said.

She sure eats a lot!

"Thanks." She said.

"Who was the other girl with you?" he asked, when she came back with another helping of rice.

That's her third helping!

"Agent Chopra. Why?" she asked.

"It's nothing big. Is she at the east gate?"

"Yeah, why? Who's with her?"

"Agent Patel."

"Oh…"

She's about to get annoyed and he's about to get beat up by her if he tries anything funny…

"What about you? Where are you posted?"

I'm not about to tell you!

"I don't know."

After they had their dinner they went to their hostels.

The next morning came. Everyone got ready and went to school. At break time, Radhika and Simran talk.

"This physics textbook looks so boring, don't you think?" said Radhika.

"Really boring. But all we got to do is pass in the tests and exams!" said Simran.

"Yeah, at least biology looks interesting." She said.

"Yes, it does!" she replied.

"I'm glad that there is no uniform." Said Radhika.

"Yeah, and I like that we get to tie our hair in whatever way we want. Saves the trouble of oiling my hair and tying braids." Said Simran.

"I wonder how Indu manages. She'll have to cut it off at some time. You did." Said Radhika.

"That was for a different reason." Said Simran.

There was a silence.

"Radhika, where were you yesterday in the canteen?" asked Simran.

"I was with Indu and where were you?" asked Radhika.

"I was at an empty table!"

"Who did you sit with?" while raising one of her eyebrows.

"Arjun." she admits.

"That guy?! Simran, didn't you hear Indu?!"

"I had nowhere else to sit!"

"Anyway, where are you posted? Tell!"

"The surveillance room and you are in the east gate, right?"

"Yeah! Don't know with whom!"

"Alright!"

"Ok fine. Let's go for class."

"Yeah!"

In the evening at around 5:00pm, Simran went outside the inner gate in front of the hostels, after waiting for everybody to go to the hostel building, and went to the surveillance room cautiously. It was very dim lighted outside to avoid attention. That area consisted of green shrubs neatly trimmed at a height, three campus pole lights which are at two extreme corners, two being at the hostel inner gate and one being at a corner of the compound wall, and a small concrete room with a window. She went around the back to find a door. She opens it and sees a guy inside.

"Umm…I'm on duty here." said Simran while entering.

The guy turns around revealing Arjun.

"You? Here?" said both of them.

"I had no idea." said Arjun.

"So did I…" said. Simran.

"What's your name?"

"Agent Simran Khanna."

"Agent Arjun Singh."

They shook hands.

"Shut the door, you don't want anyone seeing!" he said, pointing at the door.

She goes and shuts the door the comes back.

"Well Agent Khanna, here-"

"How many cameras are there here? Twelve?"

What the…she didn't even look!

"Lucky guess. Anyway, here are the cameras showing the gates, school, hostels and the school ground as well. Got it?"

"Well, that's easy!"

"It looks easy but it isn't"

"Whatever…"

"Fine…"

They begin their duty.

Meanwhile, after seeing everybody go to the hostels, Radhika sneaked out from the main school building and goes behind the auditorium building secretly. She then sneaked out the inner gate nearby. She walks past the storage building and climbs the stairs to the terrace of the gate house. She goes up and is surprised to see the agent on duty.

Oh no!

"YOU!" said both of them at each other shockingly.

"Oh dammit…" said Radhika.

"Awesome!" said Raghav.

Chapter Three – Issues arising.

Dammit! I just hate this!

Radhika thought.

"Agent Patel, right?" she verified.

"Good, you know my name. You must be Agent Chopra. You seem good like your profile." said Raghav flirtingly.

Does she keep running? What does she do?

They shook hands. Radhika shook his hand firmly that he was taken aback.

"I've read up on you too. So let's get one thing clear. You annoy me, you get punched. Got it?" she said, sternly.

If he crosses a line, I'll beat him up!

"Ok! Ok! Anyway, we have to observe the gate and security over here so that nobody can sneak inside. Got it, babes?" he said.

"Got it! And don't call me that or I'll pound your face!" she told after getting annoyed.

"I'll think about that!" he said, while loading his gun.

"Wait, what are those? They aren't normal bullets!" said Radhika, while taking one and examining a small syringe on it.

"They are rest inducing dosage bullets or as I like to call, sleepy pills. If a student or faculty sees us accidently, we can shoot a sleepy pill and it immediately makes that person sleep. When he or she wakes up in the morning, after a few hours, they will not remember anything of last night. In fact, they will only get the urge to go to the bathroom. At

that time the fluid flows out with urine and back to normal!"
Raghav explained.

"There are already things called sleeping pills." She said.

"I said sleepy pills. It doesn't matter anyway because the functions are same." He said.

"But then who carries them back when they fall asleep?" asked Radhika, suspiciously.

"If it's faculty, then one of the security. If a student, then us!" Raghav said.

"How many girls did you enjoy picking up?" asked Radhika.

This guy is top 50?! What a joke!

"A few…now you have to pick them up and give them to the matron who will take them to their room." said Raghav, smirking.

Raghav was very carefree even if he was forced in the IB by his parents. Radhika had no interest of much fun.
They both remain on duty.

Indira, while monitoring the corridors in the main school building's second floor(total six floors), bumps into a girl,

Agent Priya Desai. A bit taller than Indira with short black hair, tanned slightly and very thin. Not much strong but very agile. Passed out from the Pune base. Not top 50, test score is 41.

She is also very much temper mental and always expects too much of everything. Yet sometimes she is nice. Doesn't like change but can get used to it if it's given a chance. She's jealous of the top 50 agents in school.

"Can't you watch where you're going?!" scolded Priya.

"You should also watch where you're going! It's dark." scolded back Indira.

"Oh, you shut up."

"Fight with a better reason!"

"I'm on duty here, you can leave."

"Currently we haven't decided places yet so we can monitor anywhere."

Suddenly by phone, Indira is contacted by Aakash.

Damn, not this guy again!

"Tell!" said Indira.

"I need your help right now. Where are you?" asked Aakash.

"Why? Did you get anything?" she asked, not interested.

"Someone's here at the north gate so just get here quickly!" he ordered.

"Umm…why can't you do it?" she asked.

"I seriously need you here so come!" he said after getting annoyed.

"Interesting! You need me, huh!" said Indira, mocking him.

"Just get over here!" said Aakash.

"Ok! Fine! I'm coming!" she tells in an annoyed way as well. They hate each other, don't know why. Maybe because of their fall out. Doesn't look like they have any feeling for each other.

Wish I could shoot her…

Indira cuts the phone, gives an angry look to Priya then leaves. She walks through the school ground, out the nearest inner gate and reaches the terrace of the north gate. Aakash was standing there looking down.

"Who'd you see?' asked Indira while looking down at a car in front of the gate.

"Who is it?" asks Aakash, while pointing down.

"It's princi's car so open the gate! Stupid!" she scolded.

"Sorry! Didn't know due to her many possessions!" he replied, retorting at her.

"The cars aren't hers, they belong to the nearby army base! That's not her problem." she said.

Aakash signals the watchman and he opens the gate.

Meanwhile, there was some activity going on near the west gate and Simran catches it on camera.

"Look at this!" says Simran.

"What?" asked Arjun.

"There are a few people near the west gate. How do you fix this-oh! Got it!" she said while shifting the focus of the camera.

"You're right! Okay..." he said.

"Whatever!" she said.

"I'll contact the south gate." he said, while dialling numbers from the security patrol phone.

"What? Nobody's at the west gate?" asked Simran.

"Yeah, actually, a few agents are still yet to arrive so west gate is vacant." He said.

Meanwhile, in the Principal's office,

"Ah, finally done with paperwork!" she said in relief.

Time to check all the background information on the agents...

She switched on her tablet and started looking in everybody's files but stops at one student's file.

What the-there's barely anything in here! It's erased! I need more information!

Her assistant just arrived with files in his hand.

"Madam, I've got the reports!" he said.

"Good, I hope you had no trouble!" she said, taking them and putting them on her desk.

"No, thanks for the car. I could've gotten them on my bike, though!" he said.

"I know, but there is a lot of money going in pockets of officials when they are supposed to give it for petrol and diesel. You might as well use defence vehicles. More usage, less money to officials!" she said.

"Good point!" he said.

At the south gate there were the two most experienced agents of the lot here, Nikhil and Natasha. They both are the best agents in the school since they topped like Simran in their tests. With the help of many seniors previously in their school, theywere ready for the top 50 as well.

Nikhil Patel is the type of guy who is absolutely "Perfect". The most popular guy and certainly acts the part after his test scores. Every girl in the school would die for him. He acts like the most experienced agent of the lot and always knows what he's doing. He's tanned slightly and well built. Natasha Rai is the type of girl which every guy would love to flirt with as well. She is a stylish show off and also acts like the most experienced. She is tall, thin and fair. They passed out from the Dispur and Guwahati base.

They both were also in the school for some time and their seniors would make them do a couple of jobs guaranteeing them inside a training base so they are experienced a bit.

It wasn't allowed but they did it. They were together once but it didn't work out. It was kind of Natasha's fault as she didn't understand Nikhil. Now she was regretting that and warming up to Nikhil on permanently being with him at duty. Nikhil had made the Principal order that.

Coming back, Arjun contacts Nikhil.

"What's up, bro? Getting bored with the new girl stationed there? Or your getting busy…" greets Nikhil.

They were friends for quite some time. At least for a few years. Arjun had once met Nikhil outside the school and they have been in touch since then.

How is he my friend, I'll never know! Dirty minded idiot…

"Have you lost it?! She is totally fine! I am so not of your type!" scolds Arjun.

"Okay okay! But come on, I've heard she's hot."

"Is there anyone near you?"

"Nah!"

"Then I guess…yeah…"

"Oh, good!"

"Anyway, there are some people near the south gate! You two should go with Raghav!"

"I got it! I got it!" he said and cuts the call.

He tells Natasha and she contacts Raghav through their security phone.

"Thank goodness you called! Radhika was eating my brain!" complained Raghav.

"It's the other way around…idiot!" said Radhika as she had heard that.

"Raghav…you are overreacting! And you should get to the south gate now for help! Now!" said Natasha and cut the call.

"Ok, I'm coming!" said Raghav.

Raghav gets down from the terrace of the east gate, goes behind the storage room around the inner compound wall and heads on over to the south gate where he finds Nikhil and Natasha about to leave.

"What happened?" asked Raghav.

"Duty bell!" said Nikhil.

"And it was only a few people who lost their way!" said Natasha.

"Always have to go by protocol, huh?" he said.

"You'll realize during our missions on how much we have to follow." Said Nikhil.

"It's just no fun. Following rules, service to the nation, all that stuff…so boring!" he said.

"You shouldn't have joined if you like only fun." Said Natasha, annoyed.

"I told you…I had no choice." He said and left.

Why is he top 50, I'll never know.

It was true that Raghav was forced into enrolling for the security job since his parents expected nothing big from him. His father works in the navy. He went and he worked hard by putting his anger in training where he scored 45 to get selected for the top 50. His parents were very proud but he stopped speaking to them.

They start walking back to the hostels. They meet the rest on the way and get to the hostels. They bid good night to each other and went to their rooms. Radhika went to her room and took out the small bag which the Principal gave from under her bed and emptied it. Out came a few knives with plastic covers on them, a dagger with a cover on it, two semi automatic pistolswith the IB logo on their grips and the model name on their slides, a few small packets with each containing two or three magazines of rubber bullets, a pair of sticky gloves, a packet of small syringes with tiny yellow capsules and her IB badge. She takes out a capsule and examines it.

Hmm...this is the sleepy pill, huh. Doesn't look much effective and it should be used only in an emergency...I've heard that Princi will scold us even if it's used once also. I'll have to be careful in this job.

She also finds a small paper neatly folded inside the bag. She takes it out and unfolds it. It was the list of all the contents in the bag with a clear instruction at the end:

Use the contents wisely. Every month your bag will be checked by the respective in charge and every time a file will be given to

you in which you have to fill out the number of contents used.
If more than 5 are used then an explanation is required. When
the respective in charge hands over the file, you are to fill it up
and hand it over to your agent head who will hand it over to
the respective in charge.

After reading the instructions, Radhika put everything back
in the bag and stuffed it under her pillow then slept.

The next day, at short break, Radhika and Simran talk about
their incidents of yesterday. They were sitting in a huge room
on the fourth floor called the study hall. Students usually
go there in their free time and hang out. There were a few
windows, many small tables and chairs laid out. They were
sitting in a corner at a table near a window overlooking the
cricket grounds and the south gate.

"Do you have any idea who I was with?!" said Radhika
irritably.

"Raghav, right?" answered Simran unknowingly while
typing in her laptop.

"You knew?! How come you didn't tell me?!" she asked.

Oops…

"Sorry…it totally slipped my mind. " said Simran.

Radhika started getting angry and she was ranting on about him and the way he annoyed her.

"…And he was nonstop blabbering! And he's saying that I'm eating his brain! Can you believe that?!" she said.

"Why do you have to get angry so quickly!? It's no use!" said Simran, getting annoyed.

"But-"

"Why are you getting affected? Do you give a damn about it?"

"No…"

"Then you don't have to get irritated for tiny reasons! You don't even have to talk to him or about him!"

"Ok! Just leave that, 'babe'!"

"Gross. And I can see him!"

"Oh I didn't!"

"Where are your glasses?! You can't manage anything without them! And don't tell me that your wearing lenses! They make your eyes itch!"

"Chill out! I threw the lenses! My glasses are in my pocket and I will wear them during class! Wait! Who was with you in the surveillance last night?"

"Arjun!"

"That idiot? Whatever! Anyway, saw how many questions he was answering in class today?"

"Yeah, you don't even answer that much."

"Yeah…he's kind of cute, though."

"Think whatever, I don't care. But I cannot believe you don't know about those rest inducing pills! They were made for our usage!"

"Don't worry, after last night, I read everything and saw everything in the bag. He called those capsules as sleepy pills!"

"That's a nice name!"

"Anyway, let's go to class! I hope you did that biology homework!" said Radhika.

"Yup, I did!" said Simran.

They get up and leave to their classroom on the sixth floor after keeping their previous class's books in their lockers and taking their next class's books.

Chapter Four –
Welcome to the team!

Meanwhile, Natasha, Nikhil and Aparna chat a bit while the two of them passed by the CEC classroom.

"Hmm..." – while seeing the test score mark sheet of Simran on the IB website – "Well, 12.5 points in all parameters! The official of her base complimented her quite a lot! Passed with distinction." said Aparna, very impressed.

"I'm telling you, it's almost impossible to top the test for the top 50!" said Natasha.

"Yeah, how did she do it? I've found out that there was no other agent related to her except her father who is a friend of the Princi but you know Princi. She didn't have anybody helping her like we did!" said Nikhil.

"Guys, chill out! Maybe she really did work hard. You guys were training and hanging out with the seniors for two years. They helped you. She must be capable in shooting, combat, intelligence and agility." Said Aparna, reassuring them.

"What are you trying to say, huh?" asked Natasha.

"Yeah, do you think the seniors rigged the test for us?" asked Nikhil.

"Look, rumours among us about you suggest so but hey! I know you guys, you worked hard! Maybe she did too!" said Aparna, defending her.

"Do you like her or something?" asked Natasha.

"Don't start thinking that! You're my best friend! I'm just a bit impressed because I noticed Arjun and her talking normally. I don't know how she's even having a conversation with that guy!" said Aparna.

"Wait, did you just say that Arjun talked casually to a girl?" asked Nikhil.

"Yes, he did! Okay, here! I'll observe her in the coming weeks for you guys. I'll try being friendly to Indu since she's hanging around with her. I'll also get Shreya. Let's see her in the sports tournaments and quizzes. Okay?" said Aparna.

"Great!" they said.

Sports tournaments were held every school weekend(Friday, Saturday and Sunday) house-wise. Quizzes were held anytime during the week and a notice was given for each competition. The houses are Blue, red, green and yellow.

"But remember, Nikhil! You topped in shooting in a fluke when you really can't do it if it's needed! Natasha, you are not that strong when it's needed!" said Aparna.

"So that's exactly why I'm saying that it's not possible!" said Natasha.

The bell rang just then.

"Just check her!" said Nikhil.

"Got it!" said Aparna and left to her MEC classroom.

On the way to class, someone coming from the opposite way crashes into Simran and they both fall down. The girl whom she crashed into was another agent, Aanya, who was Radhika's roommate.

She is very kind and dedicated but doesn't stand up for herself. She also gets annoyed easily whenever someone tells her that she's weak. She was having really long straight brown hair in a braid and she had glasses on. Thin but quick with a gun yet not accurate. No one knew that. Only top 400, test score was 33.

"My mistake! Sorry!" apologizes Simran.

"No need! I was in a hurry! Hey Radhika!" said Aanya after getting up.

"Hey, Aanya!" she replied.

"Well, I'm Simran!" she said while getting.

Hmm...she's the topper!

"Aanya!" she said, giving a tiny smile.

"Well, see you around!" says Simran.

"Sure! Bye!" said Aanya and left.

They both go to the classroom just before the teacher arrives.

At the lunch break, everyone meets in the canteen and Indira starts to introduce Simran and Radhika.

"Here are the newest members of our team!" announces Indira.

"Hey Simran!" greets Arjun.

She didn't reply or pay attention to him.

Everybody in astonishment looked at him and her but Simran didn't notice that.

She was dabbling on her phone while Radhika was suggesting stuff to her while pointing to her phone.

"You both got friendly...I'm disgusted and he's a bit cute for you!" whispered Radhika with a surprised look.

"Shut Up! Don't even think about teasing!" whispered back Simran.

Radhika looks around at everybody and noticed Raghav. In a minute he noticed her as well and they both looked at each other for a moment. The moment broke when Raghav smiled naughtily and winked at Radhika. Simran notices that and gives a nudge to her.

"Ouch..." muttered Radhika under her breath.

"I see your new friend over there! It's disgusting." whispered Simran.

"Shut up!" Radhika whispered back.

"This is our team! I hope you know a few of them! Anyway, this is Arjun, BiPC, Aanya, MEC, Gaurav, BIPC, Natasha, CEC, Nikhil, CEC, Raghav, MPC," - Radhika totally ignores him annoyingly – "Aparna, Rishi, MEC, Siddharth, Priya" - who rolls her eyes at them" – ", Shreya, Neerav and Aakash, MPC!" says Indira.

"Hey!" said Simran, without looking up again.

"What's up?" said Radhika, feeling awkward already.

Many were not paying attention.

"Nice to meet you, Simran!" said Raghav.

"Good to have you both!" said Nikhil.

"Simran and Radhika...during your missions, you will join me, Nikhil, Natasha, Arjun, Raghav, Gaurav and Aakash. We are the top 50 agents!" said Indira.

Radhika walks ahead pulling Simran with her passing Arjun and Raghav and stops in front of Gaurav. When they stopped in front of him he got up.

"This is him! He's the guy, Simran!" said Radhika.

"Which guy?" she asked, confused as she looked up from her phone.

"The one at the Hyderabad base! I told you!" she said.

"Who the-Oh! Yeah! You are from the same base, right?" said Simran.

"Uh...yeah! I am!" he replied.

"Sorry, I never noticed many people. I just focused on the test. Oh, I got to fix something so you two talk! Nice to meet you, Gaurav and welcome to the top 50." said Simran and left while dabbling on her phone.

"That is my best friend, Simran! I didn't know you were selected in the top 50. That means it's three from the same base!" said Radhika.

"Yeah, I guess so!" he said.

"But you didn't come with us!" she said.

"My friends were in the jeep. And I went home then arrived in the evening yesterday." – the bell rang – "See you around... Radhika." he said and left.

After lunch, everyone were walking back to class. Arjun and Simran lacked behind them and talked.

"You're good at observing things in the cameras, not that I admire it." Said Arjun.

"Thanks, not that I care." said Simran.

"Is there a problem?" asked Arjun.

"No." Said Simran in a non interested manner.

"Okay, just good job!" said Arjun.

"How many times do you have to say that?" asked Simran.

Suddenly Radhika interrupts their chat saying "Simran, we need to talk! Now. Arjun?"

"Sure! See you!" said Arjun.

"Yeah..." said Simran.

After he leaves both of them, Radhika, in fury, drags Simran near a corner and said "Seriously! Why!?"

"What's your problem if I talk to him?" said Simran.

"Excuse me, not about that! You just left like that! It's bad manners!" she said.

"Look, my phone wasn't working." she said.

"Oh, then okay! But what do you think of him?"

"He's nice but he looks a bit bothered. Family troubles, perhaps. Trust me, I can tell. Overall, he's fine. Not like Raghav, at least!"

"Raghav and Arjun, I tell you! They are so similar! I see one and get reminded of the other!" she said.

They are definitely not the same. Arjun doesn't even wish to see a girl's face. I can tell.

"You get reminded of them this way?" asked Simran while raising her eyebrows in amusement.

"It's stupid, right?"

"Yes and you know how much I prefer logic!"

"Of course."

"Anyway, did you call your family?"

"Uh, just a quickie. Sorry!"

"It doesn't matter! I got to go! Bye!" said Simran.

"I suggest you to keep away from Arjun, though. He looks trouble and everybody else hates him. He's not nice to anyone!" warned Radhika.

"It's okay, I'll maintain distance. You be careful around Raghav too! And hang out with people like Gaurav. It'll do you good." said Simran.

"Okay, you got it!" she said and suddenly sneezed.

"You are very strong and fit but you still get sick so easily!" said Simran.

"I'm not used to this weather. I'm surprised that you are not getting this problem!" she said, wiping her nose with a tissue.

"It'll take some time for me. We just got here a couple of days ago." Said Simran.

"Simran, this isn't fair! Can't I get anything other than a cold?" asked Radhika.

"All right! I get it! You don't like being sick! Okay?" said Simran.

"Yeah! It's annoying!" she said.

"Which is why I paid for two gym memberships at the hostel from my account!" said Simran.

"Huh? Where did you get the money?" asked Radhika.

"I sold one of my guns. No big deal." Said Simran.

"What? Why?" asked Radhika, surprised.

"I don't shoot, anyway!" said Simran.

"How much were you able to pay?" asked Radhika.

"This term only. We'll figure something out later!" said Simran.

"Yeah…thanks." Said Radhika.

Radhika's family only had her parents who are not of any defence authority. But since Radhika had Simran's father to help her enter, she was able to become an LSS agent. Her family wasn't that keen on letting her go but as soon as they read the words "…schooling paid by government…", they were supportive.

Simran's family, on the other hand, was dysfunctional. Her mother had passed away due to cancer. Her father still grieves about it. He is part of the IB at the same position as the Principal but he has a desk job while the Principal is the chairperson of the LSS recruitment committee and one of the LOCKER in charges. They were friends due to their common missions as partners before the LSS became mainstream. Simran's mother was also part of their squad together.

While walking back to the hostels, Simran and Radhika still talk.

"I'm surprised that you've actually made friends with the staff here." Said Radhika.

"You should too. They may help us anytime in our duty. They know what to do even if they don't know what exactly the LSS is." Said Simran.

"Are you serious? They don't know why they are doing this?!" exclaimed Radhika.

"They know nothing of the IB or the LSS at all!" said Simran.

"Remarkable!" said Radhika.

"I'm kind of surprised that I never notice the others being friendly to them, though!" said Simran.

"None of them? Not even Natasha or Nikhil? Indira at least?" asked Radhika.

"Maybe just her!" said Simran.

"Hmm…" wondered Radhika.

"Also, Aakash was arguing with the nurse yesterday. I don't know why! Oh, also I saw Arjun coming out from the nurse's office once!" she said.

"Arjun going in there? Weird." Said Radhika.

Chapter Five — Orientation class.

After three days, in the middle of the coaching timings, the Principal called the agents for a meeting in the secret meeting room. They went downstairs to the basement of the main school building then opened a door to a corridor. It had two doors. They opened the first one to the meeting room and sat down on the benches in front of her. Simran sat down with Radhika next to her. Raghav and Arjun came in and sat down at the back. On the board behind the Principal was only a word written in bold capital letters: ORIENTATION.

Orientation is a class for the agents sent to protect the LOCKER in the respective school. It is only one class every two years (due to the shuffling and choosing of new agents for the top 400) and it's usually teaching just the basic things, like the layout of the school and LOCKER, and how to be properly undercover, disguised, etc. Here a few people know the basic patrol rules which are taught in some training camps. That is illegal, though and only a few camps function according to the code. Hyderabad was one such camp.

"I thought we missed orientation!" whispered Radhika to Simran.

"So did I..." she replied.

When everybody entered, the Principal stood up and everyone was silent.

"All right, let's start! This is the one and only orientation class with no repetition so listen carefully, jot down tips and feel free to ask doubts because you will not get any other time to! Understood?" she said, with strictness.

"Yes, ma'am!" everyone replied.

"Now, first rule of the school! No student or faculty is allowed at the gates or patrol areas. Nobody except security is allowed at the gates and surveillance room at all times! Agent Patel, you'd better watch out! Next, if you see any student or faculty roaming outside after bedtime hours, you will not go to send them back or your cover is blown! Got that? Agent Oberoi, you almost did!" she said looking at Raghav and Gaurav.

Gaurav Oberoi is very cautious and careful. A bit muscular and tough and does care for certain friends inside. He is a little arrogant but only for those he cares about. Passed out from the Hyderabad base and his test score is 46 as well.

For this matter, he had no clue in the past week. He was about to go send a student back when a security guard stopped him and went himself to send the student back.

He looked down with his black styled hair falling on his whitish face.

"Then what do we do if that situation is there?" asked Aparna. "Who do we call? Do we call somebody else or who do we call?"

Aparna Deshpande is always afraid but she stands up to someone at the right time. A bit hefty but strong. Not agile. Passed out from the Kavaratti base. Her test score is 37. Whenever she gets in a situation, nobody but Rishi Aggarwal stands for her. He's very punctual. He's also very good at his job and calm at every time. Still nobody knows why he defends her. Agile and moderately strong. Passed out from the Chennai base. Test score is 38.

"Agent Deshpande, stop worrying! Agent Oberoi, answer her question! I'm sure you've learnt what to do!" said Vijayanti. Gaurav looked up, embarrassed enough, and replied "You call a security guard or the matron to send the student back!" in a monotonous voice.

"Good! Moving on, the next rule is to never go to the patrol areas other than patrol hours! Agent Singhania, especially to you!" said Vijayanti.

He gave a slight nod.

She continued explaining the rules of patrol.

"Next, every few days the patrol areas will be changed except the surveillance. Clear?" said the Principal.

"Excuse me, ma'am! Why should the surveillance should not be changed?" asked Simran.

"The surveillance is the most important area of security. I don't trust most of you so I won't allow the security to shuffle there. Any problem?" said the Principal, sternly.

"It's all right! No problem." she replied.

She then explained the layout of the school and the LOCKER. She also explained a few school rules for every student. Here are a few:

1. Everyday except Sunday the gates are open from 3:00 to 5:00pm. Students are allowed to go out during that time.

2. On Sunday, the gates will be open from 8:00am to 12:30pm. Students are allowed to go out during that time.

3. The agents have to patrol the outer ring four gates and students are not allowed to go out the inner ring gate except during the timings of the open gates.

4. In hostels, the canteen timings for the following are:

- Breakfast is from 6:30 to 7:30am.

- Lunch is from 12:30 to 1:30pm.

- Snacks is from 4:30 to 5:30pm(optional).

- Dinner is from 8:30 to 9:30pm.

Finally, she would choose the permanent positions of the security team.

"Now, whoever I choose as the head of the team, you will have to obey that. Agent Bhattacharya, I don't want fights from you! Don't defend yourself because this past week of you all working showed me quite enough!" she said.

Siddharth Bhattacharya is absolutely temperamental and keeps fighting if he doesn't get what he wants. Tanned slightly with brownish hair. Very tall and stiff. Passed out from the Bhopal base. He already has a girlfriend in the school but she doesn't know about his job. The Principal suspects him of something but she doesn't know.

He looked up and nodded.

"Your team heads are Agent Nikhil Patel and Agent Indira Jaiswal. They will permanently be there. But you two don't keep your guard down. I can still change my mind. Understand?" she said.

"Yes, ma'am!" they said.

"The permanent agents at the surveillance room are Agent Arjun Singhania and Agent Simran Khanna!" said the Principal.

"Yes, ma'am!" they both replied.

"Now that everything's settled, the class is over! You may leave now! Agent Singhania, stay here for a minute! I have to speak to you!" said the Principal.

"Awesome! He's screwed! There is no way he can get out of this now!" whispered Aanya to Priya.

"Let's hope so!" she replied.

Simran overheard that. Radhika went out with her but Simran stopped after everyone had left.

"What happened?" asked Radhika.

"Go on ahead for duty. I'll catch up with you." Said Simran, softly while eyeing at the door of the meeting room.

Radhika nodded and left. The Principal had already closed the door.

"You have been here for two weeks only and you think you own the place?! Kicking out whomever you want?! How dare you!" she scolded.

"I told you! I will never work with them!" he said.

"That is not your choice! You gave up the times of making your own decisions ever since you joined! And the agency's policy clearly states that in these LOCKER patrol areas, to ensure equality among agents, a male and female agent is put on duty! Respect that!" she said.

"That's a lame policy! There is one thing that you cannot change and that is me working alone!" he said.

"Yes I can. I'm your boss!" she ordered.

"I can handle everything myself. I don't need help from a girl." he said.

"Yes you certainly do. I've heard quite a lot of issues you have." she said.

"Everybody has issues." he said.

"Yes, but you cannot leave those. You have a job along with school. You have to work and study. You have health issues, first of all!" she said.

"I was still able to score well in the test!" he said.

"That's one day which you prepared your body for. Every night is a dangerous one and if you suddenly have to chase someone but your health won't let you…" she started.

"Look, it's not that big. And I will go to gym every day. Just don't partner me up with her!" he said.

"Well, one issue resolved. And the second and most important is that you haven't broken contacts with your former colleagues. This is very dangerous! I won't let you meet them. They will cause trouble and havoc. I don't trust any outsider around my school." She said.

He didn't say anything and looked down.

"This is my final warning to you! If I catch you both in a fight, if I catch you meeting any former accomplice of yours, if I catch you skipping gym and if you even try to kick her out, then I will have no choice but to transfer both of you to a school in either Jammu and Kashmir or to Andaman and Nicobar. I've heard that there aren't many top 400 agents there. It's more of the Border Security Force! So watch your mouth!" she said.

BSF?! No way! They are terrible!

Simran was shocked at overhearing the last warning of the Principal after listening to their entire conversation. That was the only thing she had heard after dabbling through her phone again.

"Now leave, Agent Singh!" she said.

Just when the doorknob of the meeting room turned, Simran leaped onto a knob and held herself onto the ceiling of the corridor with the help of sticky gloves given to every top 50 agent. From there she sees Arjun storming out of the room and leaving. As soon as he left, Simran was about to get down but then she pulled herself up again because just then, the principal opened the door and left the room. As soon as she was out of sight, she slowly dropped down and left for the hostels.

These gloves are pretty handy…What the hell was that, though?!

Shreya was leaving for duty just then when she noticed Simran going inside their room and sitting on her bed.

"We have duty, you know!" said Shreya.

"Can I just stay in tonight? Just tonight? Please?" she asked.

"Anything happened?" asked Shreya.

"Please can you just cover for me to Indu?" she asked.

"Fine, but you owe me later!" she said and left.

Arjun reaches the surveillance. He peeps in and sees nobody then he goes inside. He calls up Shreya.

"Yes, Arjun!" she said.

"Where's Simran?" he asked.

"In our room. She got a cold." She lied.

"All right!" he said and cuts the call.

Meanwhile, Simran broods deeply as she looks out her window open wide with rain pouring.

Why did she threaten Arjun? What exactly did he do? And if it's his fault then why did she threaten to send me with him? I should have listened more...or was that enough?

At the surveillance, Arjun was lost in thought instead of working.

I have got to get her out...but how? Why did ma'am partner her up with me? Whatever to her, how to get her out?!

He kept on thinking. Simran was brooding too.

So that's why he went to the nurse. His health. But he scored with distinction in the test...what can possibly happen to his health? I'll have to find out since he's my partner now. I'll have to work with him now...and I've accepted that. But will he?

At the east gate, there was Raghav and Radhika on the terrace of the gate overlooking the greenery and darkness around it.

Raghav, noticing that Radhika was in an annoyed state asked "Why are you so grumpy?"

"Grumpy? No I'm not! I don't exactly feel so good!" replied Radhika and she suddenly sneezed.

"I'm sure it's because of the weather! You'll get used to it later on."

"Yeah, later on! I'm really feeling cold now."

After a minute or two of sneezing,

"That's it, I need to go to my room. It's way too cold!" she said.

"Just wait a minute! I'll be back in a second!" he said and rushed swiftly downstairs. After a minute or two he came upstairs with a blanket and instead of putting it around her he just gives it into her hands saying "Here! Hope that should be a little warm!"

"Uh… thanks!" she said and covered herself in it.

Arjun still continued to think,

I've got it! She didn't mention anything about her leaving on her own!

"Now I know what to do!" he said to himself.

Watch out, Agent Khanna. I'm the best and I will get what I want.

Chapter Six – The notice.

The next morning, during the breakfast time in the canteen, Radhika was recalling yesterday night.

"Why are you so grumpy?" Raghav had said.

"Grumpy? No I'm not! I don't exactly feel so good!" Radhika had replied.

Then she recalls him giving a blanket to her saying "Here! Hope that should be a little warm!"

Simran arrived while she was remembering him and sat down opposite to her but still she didn't notice!

"Radhika?.... Radhika… Radhika!… respond Radhika!" she said while waving her hand in front of Radhika's face and she startles.

"What?!" asked Radhika when she startles.

"Oh, nothing! Never mind! I guess, instead of worrying about your homework you are thinking about him, right?"

"I'm not thinking about Raghav!"

"I thought Gaurav! I guess you were thinking about him! It's okay! You may!" after saying Simran gets up and leaves.

Right after she leaves Indira and Aanya come and sit down.

"Hey! What's up?" asked Indira.

"Nothing… why?" asked Radhika suspiciously.

"Oh! Just wanted to ask what did you do with Raghav last night!" replied Aanya.

Aanya had a sense of fun but she was still not mixing herself with duty.

"Duty, why?" replied Radhika.

"Only duty or…" started Indira.

"Get out of my face if you talk about these things." She said, seriously.

"Lighten up, we were just teasing. It's for fun.

"I don't like fun!" Radhika said furiously and left.

Indira and Aanya, on the way to school, catch up with Simran and ask her "How were you Doing last night? With Arjun?"

"I was sick. I didn't go for duty last night." replied Simran.

"Oh yeah." said Indira.

"Will he be a pain?" asked Simran.

"Of course not. But it depends on what type of pain you mean." said Aanya.

"Disgusting! Go away, Agent Kaur!" said Simran.

"But it seems that you two were bonding! He is a pain, but I think he'll adjust with you just fine. He never talks normally to girls but maybe he got affected by princi's lecture yesterday." said Indira.

"Okay...I can adjust too." saying that Simran left.

Indu, Arjun did not get affected by that. I can tell. But I will not leave or else I will be transferred to a place where I will only have him. And Aanya, has free time only nothing else! Stupid girl...

But Arjun was coming and he bumped into her. "Sorry I" he was about to say but she just left in a hurried manner without looking back at him. He spots Indira and started asking "Did you both say anything weird to her?"

"I was, I mean, we were just teasing her!" replied Aanya, casually.

"May I ask with whom?" he asked.

"With you! Who else?" said Indira.

"Are you mad?! Don't do that! You know that she is new here so don't start teasing her from day one! And with me! How stupid! You typical girls have no other work!" said Arjun, scolding them.

"Look, I'm going because I didn't say anything." said Indira, defending herself.

She was about to go when Arjun caught her braid and pulled her back.

"Just a minute! What's so interesting here? Me talking to her?" he asked.

"Leave my hair! I have nothing against you from the time I left the surveillance. Let go!" she yelled and he did.

She immediately left.

Asshole!

"Well, yeah! It is pretty weird!" said Aanya.

"I'm telling you! Just because we talk normally since we're supposed to doesn't mean anything more than partners." saying that Arjun left angrily.

At that time Natasha entered asking "What did you do?"

"I was just teasing him with her!" said Aanya.

"Her as in Simran?"

"Yeah!" said Indira.

"Have some class! Whatever to your thoughts, just don't mess with him!" and she left.

Meanwhile, at lunch break, Simran sees a notice on the board:

NOTICE

The inter house cricket tournament on the two cricket grounds will be conducted this school weekend. All house captains are required to form a girls and boys cricket team by then for the 5-5 over matches on Friday. The schedule of matches are below:

Ground 1(Boys) –

Friday

1. Red house vs. Green house

2. Blue house vs. Yellow house

Saturday

Final

Ground 2(Girls) –

Friday

1. Blue house vs. Red house

2. Green house vs. Yellow house

Saturday

Final

Shreya came next to Simran while she was still reading.

"I knew you were into this!" said Shreya.

"No, I was just reading!" said Simran.

"You think I don't know how fit you are? How else would you have topped the test?" asked Shreya.

"I'm certainly not like you. You are definitely one of the most fit people I have ever seen!" she said.

"Thanks, but you do have a chance! I'm friends with our Blue house captain. Come on! I think you can hit!" said Shreya.

"I'm much more of a bowler actually!" said Simran.

"That's perfect! Other than me, others suck at bowling! Come on! I'll go tell your name to the captain! Please!" she said.

"All right, fine! You can!" said Simran.

"Awesome!" she said.

Anyway, in the evening, Simran was waiting near the surveillance room when Natasha asked her "Can you ask Arjun for the criminal file?" and she replied "Sure!".

After a few minutes, Arjun came with the keys running and opens the door while apologizing "Sorry I had to stay back for remedial classes-"

"What's that purple colour stuff on your hand?" asked Simran, while touching some and examining it.

"Guess yourself!" he said.

"You were doing something!" she said.

He unlocks the door.

"Be elaborate!" he said.

"No need. It's your personal-" she started.

"Just say it!" he said.

"You and Miss popular were getting close. But you didn't let her do anything!" she said.

What a slut...behind him.

"How do you know if it's her?" he asked.

"I noticed her wearing this shade of lipstick! Nobody else does. Plus, rumours in the girls' hostel tell that her latest interest is you!" she said.

"How do you know whether she did or not?" he asked.

"You are not interested." she said.

"You don't have to notice my personal stuff just because we are partners in security!" he said.

"You are the one who just told me to say this! I just happen to notice things and I don't go around telling others!" she said.

They stopped talking at that.

Impressive. She knows a lot! It's going to be hard to kick her out!

"By the way, Natasha is asking for a criminal file. Could you give it? I'll give it to her." Said Simran.

"I'll give it myself. It's an important file. I don't take chances." He said, took the file and left.

Well, what a defensive guy. I'll see all of the files one day or the other.

Meanwhile, at the east gate, Raghav wonders where Radhika was and calls her.

She picks up asking "What do you want?"

"There's duty tonight! You need to come! You have to come!" said Raghav.

"I can't! Aachoo! I have a cold!" she said while sneezing.

"But you already had one! Toughen up!"

"No! I even have a little fever and I'm fine here!"

"How bad is it?"

"It'll go on for two days!"

"Two days?! Are you kidding me?!"

"Just manage alone like you did before."

"Actually… Arjun was with me."

"Oh! Well anyway I bother you so you can concentrate without me, ok?"

"Babes, please!"

"I'll cut the phone call if I hear that again!"

"Are you sure you can't come?"

"Well, Simran won't let me out of bed!"

"Wait, your alone in your room, right?" said Raghav, hitching up an idea.

"Yeah… Why?" said Radhika.

Meanwhile, Arjun calls Raghav but the number's response was "The number which you are trying to call is busy on another call. Please try again later." He keeps calling two to three times but that message kept coming.

Raghav and Radhika continue to talk.

"I don't want to call Arjun for help. He should be relaxed!"
said Raghav.

"So what are you going to do?" asked Radhika.

"I have a plan."

"Go on"

"Where's your hostel room?"

"Why do you want to know?!"

"I'm going to have to come get you! Just jump from the
window and I'll catch you! Ok?"

"What?! Not to be rude, but you must be half of my weight.
Plus, I know how to climb down. I just don't want to."

"I don't care, either come now or I will come! And I don't
want to listen to anything! Just come now!"

"Ok fine! Five minutes!" says Radhika and gets up. She
wears flip flops and a jacket then looks down.

*I will kill this idiot. Damn, it's so cold outside. I don't want to
go. Bye for now, bed.*

She grabs her gun and phone then, with her sheets left intact, goes to her window and slowly gets down then jumps from a height. She reaches the east gate.

"Great, you made it! I-" he started but she punched his face.

"That was for waking me up from bed!" she said.

At the surveillance, Simran keeps a huge distance from Arjun while watching the cameras. Arjun notices and moves a step close to her. She doesn't notice and he takes a couple of steps and stands next to her. Then she notices and moves away a step.

"What problem do you have with me?" he finally asked.

"Nothing." she replied.

"If I get close to you then you'll just move! Why?"

"You should be happy about that!"

"What do you mean?"

"Nothing."

"Tell me!"

"What's the problem in just giving me distance?"

"I'm just a bit confused. Do you have a problem with me?"

"No, no problem! But we aren't friends so just keep your distance from me!"

"Is it the teasing? You really don't have to worry!"

"Yeah...I know."

"It's ok! You don't have to worry!"

"I know that. Are you deaf?"

"No!"

"Okay..." she said.

"Girls..." he muttered.

"I've got to check up on Radhika so I'll be right back!" she said and left for the hostels.

"Typical him..." she murmured.

On the way, she calls her.

"Radhika, I'm coming back. I finished duty early and I hope I don't find you out of bed!" she said.

"What!! I mean, yeah good I'm right here!" she said.

After putting the phone down,

"I'm leaving. Simran's coming." She said and left.

She climbed a pipe with the help of her stick gloves and entered her room through her window. She quickly took them off and took off her jacket.

At that time Simran arrived and seeing Radhika out of bed she asked, "What are you doing out of bed?"

"I went to the washroom!" lied Radhika, easily.

"Well, are you fine because I have some duty left!"

"I'm just fine, alone! You can go, like now!"

"Okay I'll just go then. See you!"

"Bye!" said Radhika and Simran left.

Immediately after she left, Raghav called her.

"What?" she asked.

"Are you done yet? We still have duty!" he said.

"Shut your mouth and do it yourself!" she said and hung up.

Simran immediately came inside.

"I knew it! You went outside! What is going on? I thought you said you didn't feel well!" she said.

"He was going to come to my room! So I just went for a little while then came back! I hate this guy!" she said.

Her phone started to ring.

"Speak of the devil!" she said and was about to lift it when Simran took it and cut the call.

"I understand." Said Simran.

"Could you just switch that off and keep it with you? If I don't get a good night's sleep than I won't be able to attend the meeting tomorrow. I have to get my place changed!" she said.

"Okay, okay. Calm down. I have this, okay? Sleep well. Even if you don't feel well don't worry. I will get your place changed. I promise!" she said, reassuring her.

"Swear?" she asked.

"Yes, I will get your place changed!" she said.

After a little more talking, Radhika went to bed and Simran left after turning the lights off in her room.

This guy is behind her. I am not going to let him do any nonsense. I will get her place changed.

Shreya and Aparna were talking in the corridor of the main school building during patrol.

"Don't you think you are underestimating her? I think she is hardworking. She never got in trouble at all!" said Shreya.

"I'm just checking. Nikhil and Natasha don't like people being better than them. Plus, after seeing the Princi have ties with her, they were very angry and they suspect partiality done. So let's see how good she does in the cricket match!" said Aparna.

"Did you actually find out anything about her? Her family background?" asked Shreya.

"Family? No, they are secret. I can't hack into computers for information. I just know that her father and Princi used to work together! But that's it! I don't know if she has siblings too! She's mysterious! Radhika, her bestfriend also doesn't tell anything. I don't know much about her too. I'm not even going to her!" said Aparna.

"She has high-tech stuff. Maybe she's a bit wealthy. She has impressive guns and her laptop and tablet are pretty cool. I never see her carrying a gun to duty, though!" said Shreya.

"Hmm...well, I'm pretty sure someone rigged that test for her! But let's see!" said Aparna.

Chapter Seven – The mysterious bomb, the cricket tournament.

The next day, which was Friday, right before going for the tournament, there was a meeting and everyone except Radhika wasn't there.

"Everything's moving pretty smooth. I'm glad there weren't any disturbances. Did any of you find anything unusual?" asked Natasha.

"Well, um…" hesitated Aakash.

"We got a tip from the police station!" said Indira.

"What's the tip?" asked Nikhil.

"There have been sightings of outsiders sneaking inside various buildings and placing..." said Indira.

"Bombs?" said Nikhil.

"But which type of bomb?" asked Natasha.

"When we find it then we'll tell you, okay?" Priya cheekily replied.

"This attitude is why you aren't in the top 50!" said Nikhil, getting angry.

"Oh, really? And the influence of seniors makes you a top agent!" retorted Priya.

"Guys, focus! The whole school will hear you!" said Siddharth.

"The room is soundproof!" they both said.

"It was just a figure of speech! Stop it!" he said.

They both stepped back. Aparna looked at Shreya and mouthed "I told you!" and Shreya nodded slightly after seeing that.

"By the way, Raghav...where were you yesterday night?" asked Aanya.

"Yeah! You weren't at the gate!" said Gaurav.

"Were you again out on a date?" asked Rishi.

"Or more than that?" said Neerav.

"I thought Princi made it clear for you to be at duty without fail." Said Nikhil.

"Hey! I was at the gate! And there was nothing there!" said Raghav and he goes out of the meeting room with Arjun going after him.

Back to the meeting, Nikhil said "Anyway, we have to change our places except surveillance, of course."

"Let Shreya and Rishi be at the east gate while Raghav and what's her name Radhika stay at the hostels. They work well together." said Indira.

"Indira, please don't. She's not comfortable around him." said Simran, softly.

"Let her be with me in the ground, then!" said Siddharth.

Priya glared at him but he ignored her.

"Good then Priya, be with Raghav!" said Nikhil.

"Let Aanya and Neerav be at the south gate, Aparna and Gaurav would be at the west gate while I and Indu will be at the north gate only. Agreed?" confirmed Aakash and with that everyone agreed.

Nikhil rolled his eyes.

It's okay, we just started. Don't beat him! That leaves me and Natasha at the main school building.

"Yeah, with your decision making self!" muttered Indira under her breath.

Meanwhile, in the end of the corridor of the meeting room, Arjun stops Raghav.

"Yesterday night I tried calling you but I got busy on my phone. What's going on?" asked Arjun, suspiciously.

"Nothing...wait! What did you think?" asked Raghav.

"You were chatting with miss popular, right?"

"No! I wasn't chatting with anyone! And I'm not interested in her!"

"Are you Raghav?"

"Shut Up! You have some problem! Miss popular is into you!"

"No, she's not!"

"Oh, she so is! Admit it! She was going to kiss you! I saw her do that!"

"She tried but I didn't let her! I hate her. She's disgusting!"

"Why? Just because she's behind every guy?"

"See, she'll be after Nikhil now! She thinks she can hit on older guys!"

"I'm kind of surprised that you are comfortable with your new partner. Maybe because she is hot."

"Yeah, think what you want."

"Whatever, anyway, Radhika didn't come for duty yesterday!"

"So you're interested in Radhika this time! Only flirting? Your flirting took quite some time!"

"Stop it! I was just talking!"

"You are saying that?"

"You'll never get me!" said Raghav, angrily.

"Forget about her. She's not interested in you!" said Arjun.

"Whatever!" he said and left.

"She doesn't even know you! You barely know her! She'll call you a creep before you know it!" he called out.

The meeting was over and everybody headed to the individual cricket ground bleachers located in the middle dividing the two grounds and settled down.

At the girls hostel room of Simran and Shreya,

"Hey, nice tracks!" said Shreya.

"Do you have an extra jersey? I only have the IB one!" said Simran.

"Sure, here!" said Shreya, while giving a jersey.

While walking downstairs to the ground,

"Do you mind telling me which groups are the agents in?" asked Simran.

"Sure! In the blue house, I, you, Arjun and Raghav are there. In the red house, Aakash, Radhika, Indira and Priya are there. In the green house, Nikhil, Natasha, Gaurav and Siddharth are there. In the yellow house, Aanya, Rishi, Aparna and Neerav are there! Got it?" said Shreya.

"Yeah, got it!" said Simran.

They reached the ground. Many people were surprised at Simran there. Many people didn't know much about her.

"Who's she?"

"It's unlike of the blue house taking new players!"

"Woah! She's hot!"

As they passed by the people at the bleachers these were mostly the comments given. They ignored them and continued talking amongst themselves. Shreya takes her to the blue house captain.

"Hey, this is Simran!" said Shreya.

"Hey! I'm Ram! I have hopes on you! I'll be watching!" he said.

"I'll do my best!" said Simran.

The time of the match came. The red house decided to bat since they expect the bowling to suck.

"All right, we will play alternate overs. You want to go first?" asked Shreya.

"How about you go first, I'm a bit nervous!" said Simran.

"Okay, I'll bowl this over!" said Shreya.

She leaves and begins. Out of the six bowls, two boundaries were hit, one was a wide and others were giving dot balls. She finished and came over. She handed over the ball to Simran and took her cap from her.

"Do your best! See you!" said Shreya.

Simran went to the pitch and went back counting her paces.

"Hey, new girl! Don't get scared, aye? I can hit on fast bowlers so forget about wickets!" said the girl on strike.

Oh really! We'll see!

Simran turned around and rubbed the ball on her thigh then started running at her and bowled. It bounced once and the girl completely missed it with the middle stump getting hit! Out! The first wicket was gone! The girl left while cursing. Another came. Simran bowled a dot ball at her. The next two balls were dot balls. The next was another wicket as Simran threw a Yorker and the ball went too high behind the batter when she hit. The wicket keeper caught it. The second wicket was gone! The last ball was a dot ball. Simran went to Shreya and passed the ball to her.

"I knew it! I feel motivated now!" said Shreya and went for her over.

She took two wickets and gave a boundary and three more dot balls. Another girl bowled the fourth over giving too many runs. The balls were one, two, one, four, four, one for her. Simran got the last over. She took three wickets and gave the rest as dot balls. The total score they made was 27-7. Their batting time came and in the first over Shreya opened with another girl. In the first over, Shreya hit two boundaries and a run till the other girl gave a run and she was bowled right there. Another girl came and she was bowled at zero runs. The second over was one, dot, dot, four, dot, one, wicket. Simran then came in the third over.

"I'm not that good in batting, Shreya!" she said.

"You will at least stay on the pitch. Don't get out! Make a run to get me on strike, that's it!" said Shreya.

Simran was on strike. She hit a dot ball.

"Yo, you got this! Come on!" said Shreya.

Simran hit one run. Then Shreya hit three runs. Simran hit another run and was close to getting a run out. Shreya hit another run and Simran hit a dot ball. The score was 19-2. In the fourth over, Simran hit two dot balls.

"Come on! It's okay! We got time!" said Shreya.

Simran hit another dot ball while the girl bowling her was taunting her.

"Come on, girl! You can bowl but not bat!" she said.

I hate these stupid bowlers...

"Don't listen to her!" said Shreya.

Simran hit a run. Shreya hit a run. Simran hit another run getting strike again.

"All right, just five more runs!" said Shreya.

"I feel great right now!" said Simran.

"All right, but be carefull. I don't want anybody out now!" said Shreya.

"Got it!" said Simran.

Simran hit a run. Shreya hit a dot ball then a run. Simran was on strike.

"Be careful! I'm there. Don't be rash! Hit a run! I got the rest!" said Shreya.

"Don't worry, newbie! I'll out you easily!" said the girl bowling.

Hmm...let's see about that!

In the next ball, as the girl came smiling, Simran hit hard!

It went high and it went over the boundary line for a six!

The Blue house won!

"I'm sorry! I couldn't resist!" said Simran.

"It's cool! We won!" said Shreya.

Natasha and Aparna noticed from a distance. Natasha thought.

Damn! Show off. I have to beat her.

Aparna thought.

Good, very good. She can definitely top!

Arjun also noticed from a distance and was impressed.

She's the topper? I could've also topped but I just got 49 on 50. She's not better than me. Not her, not Natasha, not anybody.

After the lunch break, Shreya and Simran watched the blue house's match with green house of boys in which blue house won. Arjun literally bowled four wickets at a stretch. Other bowlers bowled all the players before they reached the score.

In girls, the green house won over the yellow house. In the boys, the previous match was red winning over green. Natasha scolded Nikhil.

"Stop it. I'm not in a drive to win! Plus, I think you are worked up with Simran playing good. I think she can work hard now but I still don't like her!" said Nikhil.

"What the-no way! I still don't believe she can top!" said Natasha.

"Look, calm down! There are always people better than you in things! Accept it!" – putting his hand on her shoulder – "All the best for your game tomorrow! See you at duty!" he said and left.

At night duty, Raghav climbs up to Radhika's room window and notices her asleep. He comes inside her room and starts to look around. He notices on the left of her bed there was a table on which there was a lamp and a pair of glasses lying on it. As he picked up the glasses and started to examine them, Shreya and Aanya had come inside.

"What are you doing?" asked Shreya.

"Uh…nothing!" he said as he put them down.

"I know exactly what you are doing here. But sorry to say that we won't let you. Get out!" said Shreya.

Aanya stood there blocking the bed.

"Listen, I just want to talk to-" he started.

"Didn't you hear what I just said?!" said Shreya, cracking her fingers.

"Yeah, I heard you clearly. I'm ready to take you on." He said.

"Shreya and Aanya. You'll be late for duty!-" said Gaurav while coming in. "Well! This is a surprise!"

"Hey, Gaurav!" said Aanya.

"Gaurav, I can take this guy!" said Shreya.

"I know that but let us take this matter outside. If she wakes up…" said Gaurav.

"Yeah, she'll tell us to leave him!" she said.

"No, she'll beat the crap out of him, taking all the fun!" he said.

"Really?" said Shreya.

"She's a two time champion of her district in boxing. Trust me. I know." Said Gaurav.

"How do you know so much about her?" asked Aanya, getting a bit concerned.

"What's it to you? I read up on her!" he said.

"That's cool." – grabbing Raghav's collar – "Let's go, then!" said Shreya and dragged him outside the room with Aanya following her.

Gaurav was about to go out too after switching off the lights when he heard a voice.

"Keep them on. I will go for duty in a couple of minutes." Said Radhika.

Gaurav turned around.

"Yeah, I was awake!" she said, while getting up and folding her sheets.

"Huh, why did you pretend?" he asked.

"If he starts talking to me, it will never end. What a creep!" she said.

"Yeah…" he said.

"So you know about my boxing titles, huh." She said.

"I…read up on you!" he said.

"Good. Sorry by the way, you had to go through that trouble to get him out." She said.

"It's no big deal. He's a pathetic loser. How is he in the top 50?" he asked.

"I have no idea!" she said.

"Hmm…anyway, see you…Radhika!" he said and left.

Shreya already gave a black eye to Raghav when Gaurav reached and he started apologising. Then she let him go for duty.

"Simran was right in sending me back to check on Radhika while I was picking up my gadget log file. I still need to fill it. What a bothersome!" she said.

"I need to fill my log file too. Oh, we have to give it tomorrow." Said Aanya, getting reminded.

"Yeah…let's go for duty now!" said Gaurav and left.

Later on, at the south gate, Aparna was checking the perimeter through the watch scope and suddenly she saw a shadowy figure slip off the school terrace and sneak away!

"Gaurav!" she exclaimed.

"What! What happened?!" he asked.

"Someone! He was on the school terrace! Then He got away and"

"Contact the surveillance room!"

She contacts Simran. On the phone.

"Yeah! What happened?" asked Simran.

"Something weird is going on at the school main building terrace and"

"Okay! I'll check it out! Thank you!"

"Why?"

"I'll be able to stay away from the surveillance for a while!"

"And away from Arjun? Why?"

"He is pathetic."

"Got it! Avoiding Arjun! Update me later!" she said.

Simran cuts the phone then notices that Arjun didn't arrive yet. She goes to the terrace and starts looking around. She noticed a pile of bricks in a corner and examines them. She looks at the bottom and finds a button and she pushes it. The brick then divides into two pieces like a book. She finds a bunch of connected wires on one side and a digital clock on another which was ticking! She realized and called Arjun.

"Hey! Where did you go-" he asked.

"Get to the terrace NOW!" she ordered.

"Okay fine in two minutes-"

"No! I need you here NOW!"

"You need me?"

"Just get over here NOW!" she yelled and cut it.

Arjun was pissed. But he immediately gets up and runs to the terrace to see her trying to deactivate the bomb!

"What the HELL are you Doing?!" He yelled when he finished observing the bomb.

"Oh no! I haven't seen a bomb like this before! What am I going to do?!" she panicked.

"How much time is left?!"

"5 minutes!"

"Move!!"

"What about-"

"Just MOVE!!!!"

Simran suddenly jerked back at the sound of his voice and silently watched as he deactivated the bomb by entering codes. After it deactivated,

"It's fine! It could've exploded but it's fine!" said Arjun, with a sigh of relief, looking at Simran's frozen face while she sat in a corner. "Hey! What's wrong, miss know it all?"

"Nothing…" she said very softly.

"What's wrong?" he said while sitting down next to her.

"I just…didn't know how to do this!" she said.

"Relax, it's very rare that somebody doesn't know this!" he said.

"You love taunting me, don't you? I'm going to the surveillance!" she said and left.

He went after her and stopped her.

"Seriously, your okay, right?" he asked.

"I'm a top 50 agent who saw a bomb being deactivated. There is nothing to be afraid about! And I don't know much about bombs and how to deactivate it! So I didn't say anything! I'm not scared of it!" she said.

"Don't expect me to believe that!" he said.

"If you don't know me then that's great. But just keep one fact about me in your brain: I am never scared of anything!" she said.

"Are you a girl?" he asked.

"Well, what do you think? That I'm a boy disguised as one?! What nonsense are you asking me?!" she asked, very annoyed.

"No, it's just, I mean! Uh, leave it!" he said.

Boys...

"But how do you know the mechanism of that bomb?" asked Simran.

"I'm not telling you...it's best if you avoid telling about tonight." he said.

"No way, we have to tell about this. And you should start talking about what you did back there!" she said.

"No need..." he said.

"Since we are partners, you might as well tell me!" – Arjun said nothing – "Trust me. I can be useful!" she said.

"It's the way I would make them!" replied Arjun.

"You make bombs?"

"Well, I used to! Not anymore!"

"Okay..."

"Is that hard to believe?"

"Nope!"

"By the way, are you always like this?"

"Like what?"

"You never sound happy…"

"And you never do too. But I don't ask why!"

Huh? What's wrong with her?

"So what if this bomb was designed by you? Would you be able to figure out who put it there?" asked Simran.

"Yeah…I'll find out." said Arjun while thinking about it.

When the duty bell rang, they walk back to their hostels.

On Saturday the finals occurred. In girls, the blue house won over green house by successfully chasing 50 runs, making Natasha pissed off! In boys, the blue house lost and Arjun felt pissed off because Aakash bowled him. Right after the match, they had an argument.

"I wonder what happened, Arjun! Feeling uneasy again?" asked Aakash, sarcastically.

"Don't you start taunting me! I have no health issues!" said Arjun, annoyed.

"Oh yeah? I've heard that you were sick after the test. That's pretty weak!" said Aakash.

"You got something to say?" asked Arjun, curious.

"Yeah, I heard you hurt Indu by pulling her hair!" he said.

"Oh, so the ex speaks! She annoyed me! And irrespective of whom, I don't care about her long hair getting ruined. She'll remember not to mess with me next time!" he said.

"Oh, you don't care, huh!" said Aakash, grabbing his shirt.

"Woah…relax yourself ex boyfriend! You should stop acting like you care and mind your business!" said Arjun, grabbing his shirt as well.

Immediately they were pulled apart by their teammates.

The next day, which was a Monday, at break, Arjun suddenly realized something and immediately went to tell Simran but he couldn't get her as they had to go to the meeting room. Arjun told everyone what they had found and they were astonished.

"You mean there was a bomb!?!" exclaimed Aparna.

"Chill out! It's deactivated!" said Simran.

"But seriously, a bomb!?!" said Aparna again.

"Oh Shut Up! You've been saying that for so many times! We get it!" said Priya, angrily.

"You got to know now that she is like this!? She always reacts so much to this stuff and makes a big deal out of it and" said Aakash.

"Don't say that!!" argued Rishi.

"Shut up, Rishi!" said Aparna.

"Yeah, shut your mouth!" said Aakash.

"You know, you are making this a big deal and wasting our meeting time! Already we find it so difficult to get here without being seen and you'll just start yapping about things that don't matter!" said Simran, casually.

"What did you dare to say?" asked Aakash, in anger.

"All right stop it! All of you!" shouted Rishi.

That was the end of it. He glared at Aakash, who rolled his eyes, then looked at Simran, who mouthed "Sorry!" and looked somewhere else.

Rishi just suddenly blasted. Everyone was surprised at the way he was defending Aparna and confused Simran asked Arjun "Is there a thing between them?" and he nodded yes then said "After the meeting I have to talk to you! It's something important! Please?" and she said "Okay".

Chapter Eight – You know?

Arjun and Simran sat down and began to talk after the meeting ended.

"What's the important thing?" asked Simran.

"I think you were right!" said Arjun.

"About what?"

"The bomb's design! It is mine!"

"How?"

"Trust me, I know and they'll be back!"

I don't trust anybody! Especially not you!

"Who? Who'll be back?"

"I didn't know that they'll be back and more than ready to get me back!" he looked afraid while sitting down on the stairs when saying that.

"Who the hell are you talking about?" she sits down next to him.

"It's a very long story!" he said.

"I'm ready to listen." She said, interested.

He sighed.

"Look, just because you are my partner, I'm telling you this, okay? We are not anything like friends!" he said.

"I'm not interested in being friends! So out with it!" she said.

"I used to work in a bomb making factory ever since I was 5. Those were just for fireworks. Crazy sales would be there during Diwali for chilli bombs and hydrogen bombs. I was heavily trained in those bombs and I could even make them." He began.

"Oh! That explains last night."

"Yeah!"

"But this was just work. You were a criminal, right? This bomb was a bit complex."

Do I have to tell her? I'm going to have to. But I will still kick her out.

"There was a malfunction with some machine in the factory. It led to a huge blast of the entire building. Everything was destroyed. The insurance company didn't help in rebuilding it. I lost my father in it. He was near that malfunctioning machine. I got a few burns myself..." – pushing his sock down to reveal a few, Simran said nothing and continued listening – "I was 10 then. I did stay with my mother but she died with cancer. I had no money. I lived with my uncle since." He said.

"Hmm...okay." she replied.

"I don't remember much on how I started to make more better bombs but some people asked for help so I did. I was pretty cool as a criminal. Just making bombs and getting paid. I still have many accomplices owing me!"

"You mean that the person right in front of me used to be a bomb manufacturer and from there till now...shit!"

"Yeah! A gang found me then and forced me to work for them without getting paid. They made me blast into different LOCKERs with the help of my bombs."

"You didn't fight back?"

"No, I wasn't trained. I was just a kid. I still remember the leader who was a total idiot!"

"What's his name?" she asked.

"Brad. But the agency caught me. I passed out of top 50 training now."

"And what happened to them?"

"They've escaped and I was kept in juvenile then trained to be a top agent and I'm here now!"—he looked at her face giving no expression—"Anyway, I guess I shouldn't have told you because you're not convinced-"

"No, no it's nothing like that! By seeing the bomb I'm convinced"—sees him getting up she immediately grabs his hand—"I swear, I promise!"

"Fine! But that's it! My uncle kind of forgave me...but only him!"—he noticed her take out her hand and the bell rang—"So… if they do come here I just want you to know that those people are very dangerous and I don't need you to get hurt!"

"Me?"

"I mean, you all!"

"Whatever because I'm helping!"

"Don't! I'm not melting here by telling you this stuff! I'm serious."

"We'll talk about this later! Let's go to class!"

They get up. Suddenly Simran slips and falls on Arjun who falls on the ground. She just gets up and goes away saying "Sorry…"

At night duty, near the ground.

"Hey, Radhika…" said Siddharth.

"What?" asked Radhika.

"Raghav had a black eye! Do you know who did that?" he asked.

"Shreya might know. " she said.

"Fine!" he said.

"I heard you have a girlfriend, who is not one of us." She said.

"Yeah, everybody is having a problem with that, huh." He said.

"No, I don't have a problem. I just want you to be careful. This thing is secret enough as it is so be sure on what you are doing." She said.

"Hmm…" he thought.

At the south gate, where Shreya and Neerav were, the school car arrives and Shreya opened the gate. It came in then left out of the gate. Again after half an hour it came back.

"Neerav!" she called.

"What?" he replied when he popped up behind her.

"Open the gate! It's a late student!"

"Why can't you do it?"

"I've already opened it a few times. There are so many late students coming!"

"Why can't you do it?"

"Just go!"

"But"

"Go! Otherwise!!!!" she snapped.

"Ok! Chill! I'm going!" he said and left.

The next night, before duty, Radhika and Simran talk.

"So you are not coming to duty because…?" asked Radhika.

"I will! I mean, later! Or not…" said Simran.

"What's wrong?"

"I want to call"

"You're missing your dad? Then just tell me straightaway!"

Whatever, let her understand like that!

"Okay…" said Simran.

"So I'll see you later. Happy Birthday." said Radhika and left.

Meanwhile, Arjun goes to the mail room to check if there were any packages. He asks the mail in-charge.

"Hey! Any package for me?" asks Arjun.

"No, Arjun but I think a package came for one of your friends. Simran Khanna!" said the man, while handing the package.

"Oh! Thanks!" said Arjun and left with the package.

He goes to the girls hostel(girls and boys were allowed in each all the rooms but not after bedtime) and was about to knock the door when he hears Simran talking on the phone and listens.

"Hello? Simran?" answered her father.

"Hey, dad. Everything fine at home?" she asked.

"All good and a little better than before. I was trying to call you!"

"That's why I called you to tell you to stop it."

"I really miss you so I can't help it, *beta!*"

"I know but you know why I don't want you to!"

"I know but come on! This isn't needed! You can't stay off-grid forever!"

"I'll see about it. So anyway, I miss you!" said Simran, diverting.

"I miss you too! I've sent your gift and you should be getting it now!" said Mr.Khanna.

"Haven't I told you?! I have enough! You know I don't use them!" she said.

"Sorry! But you are great with guns and your favourite electronic stuff is too costly!" he said.

At that time Arjun comes inside.

"Uh…dad! I have to go! Bye!" said Simran, hurriedly when she was astonished to see Arjun and cuts the phone.

Arjun comes in front of her and she quickly closes the door.

"What are you doing here?" asked Simran.

"Why? I'm not allowed?" asked Arjun.

"No! I mean, you can't just pop in whenever you like! Heard what happened to Raghav?"

"We are nothing alike. Plus, you instructed them to do that!"

"No guarantee that Radhika may do that!"

"Don't worry! I have a reason, miss know it all!"

"What?"

"Some package came for you!"

"Really?" she asks and takes it.

"Yeah! So I'm going to leave now!" he said and left.

What's in here from dad?

She wondered while opening it and putting the box down. At seeing it, she sighed.

Just then, Arjun came back inside and saw the package open and Simran assembling it. He saw a tag on the box. On it was written: Happy birthday, Simran! Please don't get mad! Simran saw him and immediately got up and put the box behind her.

"You got a gun for your birthday?!" he exclaimed.

"Would you shut up? Riya, the rumour spreader, sleeps at the right of this room!" Simran said.

"If you are that worried, then I'll shoot a sleepy pill in her right now!" he said.

"No need, why are you back here anyway?"

"I forgot my phone..." he lied.

"You didn't bring one! Why are you here?" she asked as she loaded the bullets then she kept the gun in her closet with her others.

"Just like that! Your room's pretty cool, though! Princi is making sure that everybody is at duty so come on!" he said.

"Okay…" she replied, put the gun in the box and put it in her closet revealing all the guns in front of him and went with him out of the room.

In the corridor,

"Do you have a boyfriend?" he asked.

"No." she said. "Do you give a damn to have a girlfriend?"

"No…just wanted to know!" he said.

So that I don't have to deal with him when I kick her out!

"Why didn't you take a gun?" he asked.

"Guns are for those who are afraid! And I don't shoot! Never suited me!" she said.

"Then how did you top?" he asked.

Damn, why is everybody making a big deal?! I noticed Shreya a bit and Natasha was pissed off! Maybe me!

"I just did!" she said.

They stopped talking and went to duty.

The next morning, at break, Arjun pulled Simran to a side of their floor corridor.

"What? What happened?" asked Simran.

"Slowly turn around and see the young man in a sky blue shirt with black jeans..." said Arjun, softly.

She slowly turned around and saw a young man of about 20 or 22, tanned and thin with a few books in his hands. He was leaning on a pillar, looking at his watch. He suddenly looked up in their direction and Simran immediately turned around facing Arjun.

"I saw...so what?" she asked.

"Who is he?" he asked.

"He's a new math teacher for the coaching classes. Why? What's wrong?" she asked.

"I remember seeing him somewhere." He said.

"Where?" asked Simran.

"I don't remember but he's giving me a bad feeling about something." He said.

"How are you sure?" she asked.

"He said 'Hello Arjun' when I barely know him! He's giving me the creeps!" he said.

"So you are afraid of something!" she mocked.

"Oh shut up, I wouldn't be here telling you this if it wasn't serious!" he said.

"Then why are you telling me? I never forced you to!" she said.

"I just am. If we are partners, and I'm not saying yet that I accept you, but if we are partners, then we might as well keep some secrets. Deal?" he asked.

"Fine!" she said.

"So what else do you know about him?" he asked.

"He doesn't spend much time here but he roams the school building." Said Simran.

"What do we do? We can't create alarm. How do we keep a watch on him?" asked Arjun.

We?

"I'll tap his phone. It'll keep track of him. Don't mention this to anyone." She said.

"Where will you get that from?" he asked.

"I have my ways. Now let's go to class." She said and they left.

Chapter Nine – New Agents.

Later, everyone meets at lunch and Indira arrives with two new agents, a girl and a boy.

"Hey guys! We have two new agents now! Principal's orders and they missed orientation so we'll have to help them and" said Indira but suddenly Aakash interrupted.

"Just introduce them! Don't waste our time with your constant talking! God, that's so immature!" he said.

That was mean and rude. Everybody rolled their eyes at him.

"Shut Up! You are being immature!" Simran spoke up.

Everybody looked at her and Aakash gave a glare at her.
She glared back. This was one of those times when Simran's
phone wasn't working.

Arjun wondered.

Nicely done...arh! No! I'm not going to get impressed now.
Still need to kick her out since it's been a month! We just have
a few things between us as partners. That math teacher is still
creeping me out.

"This is Agent Ankita Pandey! CEC." continued Indira,
while looking at Simran.

"Hey!" everyone greeted.

"Whatever!" muttered Priya.

"It's okay! You don't deserve to be bothered!" said Ankita,
with a cool attitude.

Everyone looked at her surprisingly. Priya glared at her.

Ankita Pandey is always very straightforward and is also a
bit short tempered. She always spreads secrets when she gets
the chance. Test score is 39. Good in combat and agility.

"Moving on, this is Agent Aneesh Murthy. BiPC." Said Indira, as very little as possible.

Aneesh Murthy. Always calm and sensible. He doesn't want to get in trouble but desperate times call for desperate measures. Test score is 37. Good in combat and intelligence. Everyone greeted him as well and Priya just rolls her eyes in front of everybody.

"You both can unpack at the hostels, ok?" Indira said to them.

"Ok! Thanks, Indu!" said Ankita and left.

"Thanks!" said Aneesh and went with her.

Indira turned back to Aakash and looked furiously at him while saying "Nikhil!"

"You are with Raghav at the hostels but only for a week. Take it or leave it." Said Nikhil.

"Thank You!" she said and left and Simran went after her.

"Hey!" called out Simran and stopped Indira in the corridor.

"Thank you, for defending me!" said Indira.

"It's okay! He's a douche bag!" said Simran.

"I know! That's why I broke up with him! But he's better than Arjun!" said Indira.

She used to go out with someone like that?! Impossible! And better than Arjun?

"Arjun is confusing, but it's evident that he hates girls! Or maybe dislikes them." said Simran.

"Yeah, it won't be long when he reveals his temper!" she said.

Meanwhile, Ankita and Aneesh get to know each other on the way to the hostels.

"So where are you from?" asked Aneesh.

"Ahmedabad. What about you?" asked Ankita.

"Pune. Hey! Yesterday night, a few students came late. You know who all did?"

"That was…me…"

"That was me as well!" he replied.

They reach the hostels then Ankita goes to her hostel room and starts to unpack when Priya enters.

"YOU!" said Priya.

"YOU!" said Ankita.

"What are you Doing here?!"

"What are you Doing here?!"

"This happens to be my room!"

"This also happens to be my room!"

"Oh No!" said both of them.

"Why you?! Why?!" wailed Priya.

"It's ok! It's ok! You overreact a lot! All you have to do is stay away from me! Got that?!" warned Ankita.

"How can I stay away from you when I'm sharing a room with you?!" replied Priya.

Ankita immediately grabs a marker and draws a line on the floor from one wall to another dividing the room into two.

"You drew on the floor! That's a permanent marker! Do you know how long it's going to take to get it off?!" Priya snapped.

"Excuse me but let me explain. This is a line that divides our room into two equal parts." Ankita starting.

"So?" she asked.

"So stupid…that's" – while pointing at Priya's side – "your side and this" – while pointing at her side – "is my side!" said Ankita.

"Fine…" replied Priya.

Ankita leaves…angrily.

There was a new notice on the board which was seen after lunch:

NOTICE

There is an inter house GK quiz for classes 9-12 which will be conducted on Saturday. Those interested may go enlist their names with their respective house captains. Prepare well.

Radhika was seeing that and she heard a few of the agents behind her whispering while walking.

"Hmm…a quiz!" said Aparna.

"I'll win like last time! Nobody can stop me!" said Natasha.

"What if Simran does?" asked Shreya.

"She's smart but I think you are safe from her. She won't have much interest to participate. Although, her best friend Radhika can give a good competition!" said Aparna.

"Radhika? Please! She's just lucky enough to get in the top 50! If another base did have standard then she wouldn't have gotten in!" said Natasha.

"Nah, she scored 46. As much as I know, she got most of the score through her brains than other things. Don't underestimate her! It's mean to say that anyway!" said Shreya.

"Oh, my bad! Tough girl Shreya got her feelings hurt! I'm just stating the truth!" said Natasha.

"Oh, I got some work! Bye!" said Shreya and left, a little hurt.

Natasha and Aparna left as well. Simran came after a few minutes and stood next to Radhika.

"Hey! What's up? What are you looking at?" asked Simran.

"I'm feeling cold again. I'm going to my room!" said Radhika and left.

"Radhika!" she called out but Radhika left.

Simran saw the notice.

What happened? It's good weather today! Is it about this quiz?

Simran went after her and saw her in the hostel gym with a punching bag alone, infuriated while punching.

"Did I do something?" asked Simran, while going and holding the bag for her.

"Tell me, Simran!" – while punching twice – "Just tell me!" – while punching – "Do I really qualify for the top 50?! Do I?!" she asked, while punching the bag.

"Of course you do! You can box and you're so smart! You do qualify! What's going on, Radhika?!" asked Simran.

She stopped punching and sat down while wiping herself with a towel. Simran left the punching bag and sat down next to her.

"Tell me! What's wrong?" asked Simran.

She told the entire conversation which she heard.

"That's it! Say something!" said Radhika.

Oh, that bitch!

Simran thought that. She got up and grabbed her bag.

"Get your stuff. Now. We are going to go study!" said Simran.

"I can't. I'm lazy!" she said.

"Hence the 'We'! Come on! Go change and give your name! I'll see you in my room after duty!" said Simran and left waving slightly.

Radhika slowly smiled and left to change then went and gave her name.

Meanwhile, Aanya was going to class when she crashed into Gaurav.

"Oh! Sorry I" Aanya started.

"It's ok!" he said and left.

Radhika noticed that and started asking questions to Aanya in a free period.

"What is your history with Gaurav?" asked Radhika.

"There's very less history, Radhika!" said Aanya.

"Yes,...there definitely is. How do you know him from before?"

"Our parents are friends. Neighbours actually. We would also go to the same school."

"Oh...that's nice. I and Simran go way back similarly. We've been best friends since class 1."

"That's sweet…"

"So…you like him, huh."

"Yeah…but whenever I want to talk he's busy. Keeps on working."

"You want to talk to him?"

"Yeah…so?" asked Aanya.

"I can help." replied Radhika.

Back to the hostels, Aneesh had finished unpacking and came out then he suddenly crashes into Ankita. They both fall down.

"I'm sorry" – he saw her and immediately got up – "really" said Aneesh.

He gives his hand. She grabs it and pulls herself up.

"What happened?" he asked.

"Priya! That girl whom I snapped at! She's my roommate!" she replied, very angrily.

"Oh! Too bad, Ankita!"

"I know, right?!"

"Well, if it makes you feel better, I'm with Gaurav"

"The guy always looking conflicted and acting like he's so busy?"

"Yeah…"

"Looks like there are a lot of stuff to be learned."

"I know. The guy who commented on Indu, who knew that agents like him can be so rude!"

"I think his name is Aakash. He's mean."

"Yet he does that on purpose, doesn't he?"

"Yeah…although the one who told him to shut up was good."

"She's Simran!"

"Okay!"

"Okay…well, let's go for class." he said.

"Sure!" she said.

Later on, Radhika and Simran talk before going to duty. As they were walking, Radhika was telling her incident.

"Radhika, you shouldn't do that!" said Simran.

"Oh don't worry. I'm just getting them to talk. Nothing else." said Radhika.

"Suit yourself! Just do a favour and not tell me. I'm not into this stuff! And don't forget. My room after duty!" said Simran.

"I know that!" said Radhika.

As they were going, they stop and see that math teacher.

"What's he still doing here?" asked Radhika softly to Simran.

"Follow my lead." Said Simran.

They went up to him.

"Good evening, sir!" said Simran, with a small smile.

"Oh, good evening. I was just about to leave! I haven't seen you in my classes, actually!" he said.

"Oh, I haven't paid for the coaching classes. I have classmates telling me about you." Said Simran.

"Oh, really. What do they think of my teaching? If they told you!" he asked.

"Oh, they love it. Math is getting easier for them nowadays." Said Simran.

"That's good to know. Anyway, I have work. Lots of papers to correct. Good bye!" he said and passed them with his bag worn. Simran put her tapping device on his bag in a flash.

After he was gone,

"Why did you put that?" Radhika whispered.

"He's suspicious. He might be related to Arjun in the past. We will find out after duty, okay?" said Simran.

"Understood." Said Radhika and they both left for their patrol.

At night duty, Indira assigns Aneesh with Neerav at the South gate while Ankita is assigned with Rishi in the school grounds.

Aanya doesn't come for duty. Gaurav tries to contact her but she doesn't pick up. He asks Radhika.

"What's up?" she asked.

"You know where is Aanya?" he asked.

"At hostels. Where else?"

"Could you tell me why?"

"I don't know."

"You're her roommate! Aren't you supposed to know?"

"Is there a problem?"

"Her attendance-" he started but Radhika cut him off.

"Listen. It's just one night. She'll be there tomorrow. Ok?" she said.

"But" he started and he couldn't hear anymore because Radhika had cut the phone call and returned to her duty post with Aakash.

"You're literally so disturbing! Always on the phone! God!" he started.

"Did I say anything to you or about you?! No!" she said.

"Whatever! Don't you get on my nerves!" he said.

"What's bothering you?!" started Radhika.

"Nothing! And you don't have solve everything you see! Got that!?" he snapped.

"Well, since it's concerning me, I will! Don't think you can just shout on like that!" she scolded.

"You girls-"he started.

"Shut up!" she said and he said no more.

Chapter Ten – Jealous? No!

In Simran's room after duty, they both were sitting on her bed. Simran dismantled her laptop and layed out everything on her bed.

"Put it back together and name each part you assemble. Then we'll do something else tomorrow!" said Simran.

"Are you sure Shreya isn't here?" asked Radhika.

"No, she said she had a date! She wouldn't tell me anyway and I didn't ask either! Go ahead. Start!" said Simran. "You are going to beat her! People, like us, remember a lot. You know that!"

"Yeah, you're right!" said Radhika.

"I'm glad you didn't punch her in the face!" said Simran.

"I wanted to kick her but I remember what you said: No hurting recklessly!" said Radhika.

"When you win, she will feel the punch anyway! Okay, start!" said Simran.

She began putting back the laptop together while cleaning it and she named each part too. After assembling it, Simran turned it on and it worked like new! They then connected to the school wi-fi and surfed through the internet and logged onto the school website. They checked the faculty list.

"What makes you think he knew Arjun?" asked Radhika.

"Arjun himself has a doubt about him. I said I'll find out. Keep telling me from your phone on his whereabouts." Said Simran.

"He's at the guest hostel along with the other faculty. How long will these people be here? The coaching faculty?" asked Radhika.

"Another month. Then they leave and after two months they'll come back." – finding something on the website – "See here. He has a Bachelor's degree in math. He has three years of experience. That's all I can get now. The school server is not safe to browse more." Said Simran and closed the laptop. Just then, Shreya came in and saw them.

"Hey, guys! What's going on?" asked Shreya.

"Are you sure she went out on a date?" asked Radhika, while seeing Shreya wearing a simple jeans and a fitting t-shirt.

"I and him are simple people! So clothes shouldn't matter!" said Shreya.

"That's good!" said Radhika.

"So you are preparing for the quiz! Good! Natasha will be surprised!" said Shreya.

"She should! Anyway, it's late so see you!" said Radhika and was about to leave when Shreya grabs her hand.

"What's this black stuff?" she asked.

"Uh..." Radhika couldn't answer.

"We were cleaning my suitcase a while ago so she got some grease from the wheels!" said Simran, saving her.

"Okay! Wash properly! Good night!" said Shreya.

"Sure!" said Radhika and left.

That was close! Thanks Simran!

The next day, Gaurav almost catches up to Aanya but she sees Aneesh and goes to him.

"Hey! All cool?" asked Aanya, for verifying the plan.

"Yeah! So Aanya, right?" he asked.

"Yeah!" she replied.

The start talking. Gaurav was wondering and the rest of the day went like this. At night duty, Aanya didn't come again and he tried to call Radhika to ask why she didn't come for duty but she cuts his calls. Aakash gets bothered.

"Who is continuously calling you?!" he asks, annoyed.

"What's your problem?!" she replied.

"Is it Raghav?"

"Aanya didn't come so Gaurav is bothering me…"

"Such a girl and he is just never going to tell her that…"

"I don't think so. He looks bothered all the time. You think Indu's like that? No wonder!"

"Of course she is!"

"No! She hates you like hell because of what you say!"

"You don't know anything about what happened between me and her!"

"Care to tell?"

"Oh, no way! I swear, you and your Simran are just so nosy!"

"Be fortunate that she won't beat you up." said Radhika.

"Yeah, I should be afraid of the unknown topper!" he said, sarcastically.

"Yeah, since you aren't!" she said and he shut up.

The next day, Aakash quickly pulls Indira by her hair into the storeroom and closes the door.

"What do you want now, Aakash?! Get your hands off my hair!" said Indira.

"I just wanted to say that I know you keep thinking about me and I actually think about you too! But I just think! Nothing more!" asked Aakash, letting go of her hair.

"What's your point?"

"My point...well, if you want then I can consider being nice to you! But I mostly still hate you!"

"Again I'm asking, what do you want? You have some grudge against me to let out?"

"It's not a grudge. It's just pure hatred! If you knew the difference that time then we wouldn't have broken up!"

"I left for the right reasons! Just say what you want from me!"

"Be nice to me!"

"Friendly?" she asked.

"No, just nice because if you don't then everybody will come and start bugging me about you! So be nice!" he said.

When can I pound him? He's so infuriating! And why do people keep pulling my damn hair? I'll do something about that later.

"I don't think so!" she said and went out of the storeroom then started walking down.

He started to go after her when he fell down. She turned around and stood in front of him giving her hand. He was about to grab it when she immediately pulls it back saying "Nobody will able to work with an idiot like you. Certainly not me." and left with him on the ground.

She meets Simran later. After telling her everything,

"Well, that was nice!" said Simran.

Well, that was despicable!

"I've handled worse!" said Indira.

"Like who?" asked Simran.

"Arjun. You'll get it later, friend!" she said.

"Sure!" said Simran.

Yet, it's surprising that he didn't show any issue with her! But Arjun definitely isn't worse than Aakash!

Meanwhile, as Aneesh and Aanya were talking in the hall at one table in the centre, Gaurav was sitting with Radhika at another table nearby and noticed them once but did not look.

Can she stop this? It won't work on me!

"You should talk to her instead of interrogating me!" said Radhika when she noticed.

"I won't! Raghav shouldn't have made her do this!" he replies, very bothered.

"Do what?"

"He is giving her false hopes. I'll kill that fellow if it's the last thing I do! I do not like her! She was just a neighbour behind me!"

Ha, I knew it! What else could explain that evening in my room?

"Okay…so you feel nothing for her!"

"Nothing, I have nothing for her!"

"I know, I wasn't asking that! You always look bothered."

"I just have personal problems. And I am not interested in her. She's just a colleague to me!"

"I can see that. Shouldn't you tell her?"

"No, my parents will then scold me that I'm being mean to her!"

"Technically you don't need them anymore! Work well as security and you get a job! A paying one with house rent! Just mentioning!"

"I can't even get her alone even if I want to tell her!"

"Does that stop anybody? You have to tell her!"

"I just respect her! Not that!" he said.

"In the situation, she thinks more than that! Anyway, see you at duty." she said.

"What?" he asked.

"Places are rearranged and I'm with you at the north gate. Weren't you listening in the meeting?" she asked.

"Oh, right! See you!" he said.

Wow, she understands me!

"Bye!" she said and left.

The next day, Ankita arrives at school when she sees Aneesh finish talking to Aanya and Aanya leaves. Aneesh comes to her.

"What was that? Gaurav's going to get angry!" said Ankita.

"It's okay. Now you will see how Radhika's plan works for them!" he said.

"About time…" she said and they left for class.

Aanya was on her way to class when Gaurav immediately grabs her hand and pulls her into an empty meeting room then closed the door.

Radhika notices and sneaked behind them. While hiding outside the meeting room, Raghav spots her.

"What are you Doing?" asked Raghav, a little loud.

"Shut up and go that side!" said Radhika.

Now see how you fail...

"Gaurav? Aanya? You did this?" said Raghav.

So that you are taught a lesson to keep out of people's business. I've already learnt mine!

"Yeah!" said Radhika.

"I've been trying so hard and you just...I'm so jealous!" he said.

"Just listen!" she said.

So that you don't bother them with this stuff anymore!

In the room, they start talking.

"Sit." he said, coldly.

She sat down on one of the chairs of the conference table and he sat on the table facing her.

"I was on my way to class when you pulled me. Why?" she asked.

"You tell me!" he said.

"I don't know. You start!"

"What's with hanging out with the new guy?"

"Nothing. He missed orientation so I was filling him in!"

"Oh really! Good, you made a new friend!"

"What's your problem with it?"

"I have no problem. You should make new friends."

"Really?"

"Yeah…"

"You want to say anything else?"

"Yeah, why were you hanging out with him?"

"I wanted to make you jealous!"

"I didn't get jealous."

"What? But-"

"Look, I don't want to hurt you but I know what you feel about me."

"You do?"

"Yes, you like me. But I'm sorry to disappoint you. I don't like you in that way. Please don't feel bad. This isn't to hurt you! And I know that you can't get over this so I'm giving you permission to keep your distance from me! All right?"

"Oh..."

"I'm really sorry but it's for the best!" he said.

"No, it's fine. It's cool. I'll be totally fine. I'm happy that you care as a person. And thanks. I actually will need to stay away from you for a while, though! Thanks!" she said, acting like she had no problem when deep down, she was heartbroken, and left.

Raghav left and Radhika went in the opposite direction.

Chapter Eleven – GK Quiz, the raid.

At night duty, at the North Gate, Radhika stood there and Gaurav came and stood next to her.

"Hey, how did it go?" she asked.

"I told her. She took it well in front of me." He said.

"That's good..."

"It's not, my parents might call me anytime!"

"Don't be afraid of them!"

"Thank you...for understanding!"

"You're welcome. You still have problems, though!"

"Yeah but it's personal."

"I know...I was just saying!"

"Okay..."

"You want to be friends?" she asked.

"Sure!" he said.

Meanwhile. assigned at the hostels were Priya and Siddharth. Priya checks the terrace. She noticed a pile of bricks in a corner and examines them. She looks at the bottom and finds a button and she pushes it. The brick then divides into two pieces like a book. She finds a bunch of connected wires on one side and a digital clock on another which was ticking!

Oh no!

Remembering Arjun's and Simran's incident she immediately contacted them. In a minute or two they both arrived with Siddharth.

"What happened?" asked Siddharth.

"There's another bomb here. Who deactivated the last one?" asked Priya.

"I did. How much time left?" asked Arjun.

"Three minutes!" said Priya.

Arjun immediately goes and deactivates the bomb and takes it in his hands.

"How did you do that?" asked both of them.

"Long story…" said Arjun.

"Yeah, we'll hold a meeting and say tomorrow!" said Simran.

The bell rang. Everyone left towards the hostels and Simran and Arjun went down the stairs.

"Anything on the math teacher?" asked Arjun.

"I should be asking you that. But nothing. He just comes here then goes back. Nothing else. Did you remember anything?" asked Simran.

"I think he once did business with me in Ludhiana. I don't remember which bomb models he bought from me. Maybe the one of last night. I'm still not sure." He said.

"Did you keep records of buyers?" she asked.

"I was a kid. But I kept logs in a notebook. Yet that is of no use. It just consists of names, phone numbers, the bombs they bought and how much. No photo." Said Arjun.

"Anyway, don't worry about it. I'll fix this myself."

"Yourself? It's concerning the school so I will have to help you. Plus, Princi isn't there either." She said.

"No need. You've helped me enough." He said and left.

The next day, the quiz was about to start. In the individual selection, Radhika already impressed everybody and they instantly liked her. So did Riya. Everybody went to the auditorium and settled down. Backstage, Indira took Radhika to the red house captain, Riya. Also known as miss Popular.

"Hey Riya! This is Radhika!" said Indira.

"Oh, hey! Everybody's talking about your brains! You could name all 206 bones of the human body!" said Riya. "I'm impressed!"

Well, I don't care about you! All of my class hates you! But whatever for now!

"Thanks!" Radhika replied.

"Anyway, are you ready? It's a five member event! Your team is You, Indira, Aakash, Rajesh and me! Okay?" said Riya.

Her too?! Damn!

"Great!" Radhika said.

In the audience, Simran sits with Shreya while eating a packet of chips.

"You should eat adequate not so much!" said Shreya.

"I'm hungry! It's just a packet of chips!" said Simran.

"I'm surprised that you never get fat!" said Shreya.

"Yeah, maybe because I'm not lazy." She said while munching.

Just then Arjun arrived and sat down behind her with Neerav.

"What's up, miss know it all?" greeted Arjun from behind.

"Hungry for trouble, Arjun? There is a snack bar outside!" said Simran, munching a few chips.

"I think I just saw you eat another flavor..." he said.

How much is she eating?

The quiz began. Each team started answering one by one. The round ended and the final two teams were the red team and green team. Natasha was surprised at Radhika and

Radhika smirks at her. The final round ended but it was a tie. The quiz master spoke then.

"Now the special tie breaking round will commence. Each team has two minutes to discuss and send their best member forward!" he said.

"Natasha's going!" said the green house captain, Surya.

"Guys, let's send Radhika this time! She's going to win it!" said Indira.

"What about me? Guys, I can take her!" said Riya.

"Riya, Indira has a point! Radhika can do it! Plus, you kind of suck! Go Radhika!" said Aakash.

What? He said that I have a point?!

Indira thought that.

This guy's actually right for once!

Radhika thought that. She went forward.

"I will ask one question and whoever can answer will gain the win for their team!" said the quizmaster. "Understood?"

They both nodded saying "Yes, sir!"

On the screen behind them a picture was shown on the screen behind them. It showed a zoomed image of a part of the CPU of a desktop computer and a white arrow pointed at a set of multi coloured wires connecting one panel to another.

"Why do the wires have different colour plastic covers?" asked the quiz master.

That's easy!

Natasha didn't know!

"Wires are of different colors so as to distinguish between live wire, neutral wire and earth wire. They are of three different colors: live wire in red color, neutral wire in black color and earth wire in green color. Also to distinguish between wires of different phases or circuits, of course!" said Radhika.

Everybody was surprised. Especially Natasha.

"That's correct! The red house wins!" announced the Quizmaster.

"Yes! Yes! Yes!" they all cheered.

At lunch time, everyone assembles in the meeting room and listens to Arjun's story, although he just told about the gang, nothing about the factory and his family.

"So he did it!" said Nikhil, realising.

"Will they come here?" asked Natasha.

"Based on their signature...what is it?" wondered Nikhil.

"It's this! It's my bomb design with their logo on it." he said and he shows the brick.

There was a logo on it saying 'Kapoor Enterprise'.

"That's a manufacturing unit for arms!" said Natasha.

"So we should be prepared, anytime." said Raghav.

"Let's do it!" said Neerav.

"No! You can't involve in this!" said Arjun.

"Not again..." said Simran.

"Arjun, as much as you're risking for our welfare we're going to the same!" said Indira.

"She has a point! We're a team!" said Aakash.

Everybody including Indira stare at him in wonder.

"Try to understand, guys!" says Arjun.

"Don't Arjun! Just don't!" said Simran.

"Please just" started Arjun but Simran cuts him off.

Uh, this idiot!

"No, wait! It doesn't hurt if you listen! I know, you think you're a hero or something but you're not! So I don't care what you think about me or any other girl but I will help and you can't escape that! We all are a team and since it's regarding the LOCKER too we all have to come in. So deal with it!" Simran snapped.

Why is she so complicated?!

Everybody wondered at how Arjun was afraid of her temper and was silently listening.

"By the way, we should inform the Principal, right?" asked Siddharth.

"She's not here, she went out of town!" said Gaurav.

"Great, we're on our own! What to do? If they are armed?" asked Aparna.

"We don't have real guns either." Said Siddharth.

Shreya immediately turned to Simran, who doesn't look up from her phone.

"Hey Simran!" whispered Shreya while everyone was debating.

"Don't say anything. We are not going to use my guns. Only I have a licence for them and I won't let anybody near those. So leave out this discussion. We'll do something else!" said Simran.

"Okay..." said Shreya and Simran got up and left.

At night duty, in the surveillance room while Simran looks at the cameras Arjun starts asking.

"I'm confused!" he says.

"About what?" asked Simran.

"About you wanting to kill yourself!"

"I'm not going to kill myself! You certainly do, on the other hand!"

"Nobody cares or what?"

"Nobody does and I'm not going to kill myself!"

"You will regret that. You'll be in the infirmary and I will say 'I told you so'!"

"It'll be the other way around if you were alone! I know how to help in these things!"

"No, you are a girl! And girls only care about themselves and they only create trouble!"

"So that's your problem! Well, I don't care what you think of me because next time you need help, don't ask me!"

"I just don't need any of you to get hurt since it's my business!"

"See? This is what happens when you don't hide yourself well from those people!" snapped Simran.

Shit, he doesn't know that I know...

"Wait, what? What did you say?" he asked.

He suddenly notices people entering the school ground through the inner gate near the parking lot. Simran sees too. Immediately Arjun runs out of the surveillance room, closes then locks the door and goes. At first, she checks her phone to track the math teacher which showed him in the ground! She hears the sound of the bolting of the door and runs towards it.

"Oh no!!!!" she shouted out but nobody was there.

"You stay there! You'll only be a problem!" said Arjun.

"You liar! That math teacher is with your former gang, isn't he?!" she shouted.

"You pick up well, Agent Khanna! But I'm not letting you out! I got this on my own!" he said and left.

"Hey!!!! Let me out!! Arjun!!" shouted Simran.

Shit!! He used me!! How the hell did he know about my ways?! Asshole!!

She tries to open the door but it doesn't.

I'm going to kill him!

She tries hitting it open but still it doesn't budge!

Meanwhile, Arjun goes to ground where the gang was standing. Brad comes to the front.

"Stop right there!" shouted Arjun, pointing a gun at the leader.

The gun! That was definitely from Simran's closet! He stole it!

"Arjun! Long time no see, man!" he greets.

"It's been five to six years!" replied Arjun.

"Still haven't lost your memory! Didn't the NIA wipe it?"

"I didn't go there...you still haven't lost yours!"

"Still have your humour. You've gotten big and you've been working out!"

"Don't flatter me!"

"Wasn't thinking of it! So I would like the LOCKER codes and you will get them for me!" said Brad.

"Not this time!!" he said furiously.

Immediately, some guy from behind came and hit him and Arjun dropped the gun and fell. He turned to see that math teacher, who grabbed the gun and clicked! It was empty! After clicking it a couple of times, he realised and threw it away! Arjun immediately got up and pounced on him and the others attacked too!

Meanwhile, Simran keeps on hitting the door and finally after many attempts she busted it open! She contacts everyone to the ground and they came within seconds. She also contacts the nearby police station then kneels down to rest due to getting bruises on her arms. Radhika arrives running from the South Gate towards her while everybody else went in the direction of the ground.

"Your arms! What happened?!" asked Radhika.

"I had to break the door because he locked me in!" she said, getting up.

"Where do you want to go? You can't fight in this condition!" said Radhika.

Simran pulled out her gun but Radhika takes it and hands her a knife.

"You know you don't want to! I won't let you! Go to the infirmary. Stay with your nurse friend. And fix up anyone if they come by!" she said.

"Thanks, Radhika!" she said.

Simran left towards the infirmary which was in the hostel ground floor while Radhika went to the ground. The matron was there, who knew Simran.

"Simran!" she exclaimed.

"I'm going to the infirmary, keep this place on lockdown!" she ordered and left to a room.

She opened a door to a large room with three to four chairs and beds. The nurse was sitting at her table and she got up as she knew Simran too. Simran tended to make friends with the staff just in case.

"Sit down. Don't worry. Nobody will hurt you here." She said and Simran sat.

Siddharth hadn't noticed someone, who was about to shoot him but Priya caught the bullet on her arm instead.

Indira saw the shooter and stunned him with another bullet. Siddharth drags her inside a room and takes her to the infirmary where he finds Simran and the nurse. The nurse immediately got up and grabbed a box then rushed towards her.

"Ah!! Careful!" she said as it hurt when she sat on a chair and the nurse was tending to her wounds.

"Shut up!" – while she took out the bullet – "What were you thinking on taking that bullet?!" he said.

"You should try it sometime! Ah!!" she said.

"You should've let me take it!" he said.

"Oh yeah! Ah!! It wouldn't hurt you, would it! Ah!!" – she finally took out the bullet – "Oh wait! It would!" said Priya.

Stupid girl!

"Hold still! I'm finished!" said the Nurse.

"Good! Thanks!" said Priya.

"Stay here! I'll get you later. Okay?" he said.

"No need. I'll go myself later." she said.

"Nope, I'll get you." He said.

He leaves. A few bad guys did come to attack her but Simran went out and wounded everyone of them with that one knife. Priya was astounded. She came back inside, washed her hands in the sink then sat down on a chair while wiping her hands. The matron came and dragged the wounded men out to the ground.

My god! What is she made of!

"Priya, what bullets are the team using?" asked Simran.

"The rubber bullets. It gave us time. Have you killed before? Sorry...shouldn't have asked." Said Priya.

"No, I haven't. I only injured." Said Simran.

She left after some time, leaving Priya alone with the nurse.

A while later, the fighting noises died down and the gang was apprehended by the police who came just in time. They then handed them over to the nearest army base.

Siddharth comes back after that.

"Hey!" he said.

"Let's go!" she said and they start walking towards the hostels when they see Arjun and Simran arguing. They hide behind and near the bushes.

As they listen,

"I warned you before!" said Arjun.

"You just think you are the best and nobody else can be! Are you insane?!" scolded Simran.

"Just let the matter go! It's solved!" he said, in annoyance.

"Yeah, after I called the police! After I called the others down! Plus, you locked me in the surveillance room! I had to break the door open!" she scolded again.

"I won't do it again! Relax!" he said, really not meaning it.

"And you stole my gun!" – snatching it from his hand –

"Thank goodness it wasn't loaded! I'm seriously going to"

"What will you do?! I told you stay there! Now you broke the door! How will that get repaired now?!"

"You are worried about that good-for-nothing door instead of your life or this job?!"

"I don't care about my life or this job ever since I had to be with you! So yes, I will say about the door because we have to pay for it!" said Arjun.

Simran lost it! She grabbed his jacket and pulled him close then punched him once and kicked him! At that, he fell down. His jaw started bleeding a bit. She kicked his stomach again!

"That was for locking me up and stealing my gun! And I don't even want to see you ever again! Got it?!" she said that and left without an answer.

Ah! Damn her! That didn't get her out! Ah, she kicked so hard!

Arjun feels his face with blood coming out because of her punch while he gets up.

She and he go in different ways. They both come out of their hiding places.

"She hit him!" said Siddharth.

"Really hard!" said Priya.

"Thank god we are just friends!" he said.

"Yeah, and be happy. Your girlfriend won't fight you like that!" she said.

After reaching the hostels, Priya goes to her room and crouches on her bed.

Ankita enters seeing her.

"What happened?" she asked.

"Why do you care?!" asked Priya.

"Because you look like you have been hit again!"

"I like Sid-"

"Siddharth? Did he say no?"

"He only likes me as a friend. I didn't even tell him and I never will. He already has a girlfriend."

"Don't worry! I think you should just move on! Focus on school and duty." said Ankita.

"Really?" asked Priya.

"Yeah!" she said.

They both went to bed.

The ground was immediately being fixed by the cleaners and workers. A few students came out but went back to their rooms after seeing nothing there.

Meanwhile, Neerav and Arjun talk while Neerav fixes his wound at their hostel room.

"She's strong…this is why you shouldn't underestimate her!" said Neerav.

"You didn't have to help me. I know how much you hate me!" said Arjun.

"Yeah, I do. But I don't want blood all over the room. You know I am a bit of a clean freak!" he said.

"Oh, yeah!" he said.

"So, how many hits did you get before?" he asked.

"Quite a few. The first from a girl. Although I don't think she is one!" he said.

"Huh? Why?" he asked.

"She's tough and not afraid! No matter what!" he said.

"It looks like she'll be sticking around with you!" he said.

"What?" he asked.

"So she is definitely going to hate you for a while…" said Neerav.

Like I care!

"Yeah! How bad is it?" asked Arjun.

"You would've gotten a dislocated chin! She gave a controlled hit! Your tummy may still hurt. Are you sure you don't want to go to the nurse?" said Neerav.

"I'm fine. That's not required!" said Arjun.

Chapter Twelve – Arrogance at its limit.

The next day, in the early morning, everybody met in the meeting room before school hours.

"Well, good job about yesterday, everyone." Said Indira.

"Good job? Are you serious, right now?" asked Nikhil, angrily.

"What's the issue? The LOCKER is safe." Said Indira.

"This wouldn't have been an issue if these two" – pointing at Arjun on one end and Simran on another end – "had informed me before. That first bomb incident happened when Princi was here, she could've done something that would prevent the fight and mess after the fight in the ground! But no! You, Arjun, just have to keep everything secret and fix things by yourself. And Simran over here… do not get me started!" he scolded.

"Don't then. Nobody's asking you to." Said Radhika.

"If it wasn't for her, Arjun would've done something even more reckless. You are just overreacting because on that night, she was the one giving orders to everybody!" said Priya.

"It's nothing like that. She also kept it a secret. It's her fault too." Said Natasha.

"Exactly, it is her fault too!" said Aakash.

"Just a bit. At least, unlike all of us arguing with one another, she actually helped us work together and now we won't get busted. So thank you, Agent Khanna!" said Gaurav and left the meeting room.

Everyone realized the point of truth he made and kept quiet in anger still. Simran had left and Radhika left too.

"That concludes the meeting. Everybody can leave!" said Indira and left.

Simran was walking in the corridor when someone pulls her into a small storeroom and closes the door. It was Arjun.

"Oh no! Not You!" said Simran.

"Yeah…me! Listen!" said Arjun but she cut him off.

"I told you!! I don't want to see you! So just"

"Please!" – he closes her mouth when he saw a teacher pass by. When he left then he pulled back his hand – "Listen to me! Just this once! And please don't shout!"

"Talk…fast!"

"I'm sorry! I really didn't want anybody to get hurt! And if you want then give me another hit! I deserve it! You know that I won't do it again and-"

Is he faking? Or he was just trying to be heroic? This guy's confusing!

"Shut up!" – she closes his mouth when she saw another teacher pass by. When she left then she didn't take out her hand yet – "Okay… just wait!"

She takes out her hand and turns his head towards his right where he got hurt.

"I really can't fix what I did!" said Simran.

"Nobody's there outside! Let's go!" he said.

They both went outside.

"You said that you can't fix it?" he asked.

"Yeah…" said Simran.

He suddenly punched her and she fell to the wall then down on the floor. He then kicked her once for her to stay down.

Ah! I can't scream! It hurts! I can't even get up! Damn, it hurts! That can't be his fist…a lot of blood. Damn him!

"Looks like that fixed me! Nobody dares to even beat me and if they do…that happens!" he said.

"Your so called apology…you're an arrogant idiot, you know that? Tempermental…" she said, while getting up and limping away.

He acted all this time! But for what? To kick me out! Ah! It hurts! I should've known!

So did he.

That's what she gets! If that doesn't make her leave, I don't know what will! Ow...this still hurts!

The bell rings and everybody came out of their classes. The first to come was Neerav and Gaurav. They saw Simran, with one hand on one side of her face where Arjun hit and her tummy where he kicked, run to the empty meeting room down near the LOCKER and shut the door. They follow her and go into the meeting room to see her hand filled with blood!

What the...

"Who the hell did this to you?!" asked Neerav while Gaurav frantically opened a drawer of the projector table and took out the first aid kit while seeing blood dripping out.

"Ask your roommate!!" she snapped while Gaurav dressed her wounds.

"Are you telling me that Arjun did this to you?!" asked Neerav.

"Yeah!" said Simran.

"Why?!" asked Gaurav.

She told her incident of last night.

"He locked you in the surveillance room?!" asked Neerav.

"Yeah…" she replied.

"You beat him first?" asked Neerav.

"Yeah…" she replied again.

"And he beat you a while ago?" asked Gaurav.

"Yeah! His ring did most of the damage! That hurt!"

"His temper is too much! He's gone too far!" said Neerav.

"I thought that he usually did this!" said Gaurav.

"Hit people? No! He would be so bossy! In fact, whoever you see at duty are there because of him! I was surprised that he listened to you but I guess in this way, he hurt you more!" said Neerav.

"I'll beat him up later on." Said Simran.

Neerav gaped at that.

After what he did? Is she kidding me?

"No! You shouldn't! I know him! He'll think that you will be a coward and change your post at duty." Said Neerav.

"Hence the 'beat him up'." She said.

"Neerav, I got this. I think you should go! People might wonder where you are more than us." Said Gaurav.

"All right, Simran. Please don't do anything stupid." Said Neerav and left.

"Yeah!" she said.

I knew it. Stupid asshole! Those girls were right!

"So the fight was real…but he took advantage of it! He knew that I would be in the surveillance all along!" said Simran.

"Yeah, I think he also knows about your other abilities." Said Gaurav.

"Other abilities?" she asked.

"I'm not a fool. I know you don't shoot. I know about other things you and Radhika do." He said.

"Oh…" she said.

"It's okay, I won't tell." Said Gaurav.

He finished dressing her wounds.

"So now what?" he asked.

"I will not change my post!" she said.

"Nice idea but if you get hurt again like this-" he started.

"He doesn't know me! I'll take my chances." She said.

What the-is she crazy?!

"Are you sure?" he asked.

"I'm sure! I'll show him who he is going to deal with!" she said.

"In that case, if you need help...I'll be there, okay?" he said.

"Okay! Thank you!" she said.

"Anytime, Simran! So this makes us friends!" he said.

"Yeah, sure!" she said and the shook hands.

They come out of the meeting room and go to the hostels. When they reached,

"See you before duty! And your welcome for not getting us busted." said Simran.

"Your welcome for fixing that. Are you sure?" he asked.

"Yeah! Act as if nothing wrong happened!" she replied.

"But I won't do it for long!" he said and left.

By the way, Neerav Sharma is a good and understanding person but when nobody listens then he would threaten them to do what he asks. He does his job very seriously.

He shows concern, yet only for formality. Black hair, not styled, a bit strong. His score was 41 and he scored more in intelligence and combat.

At night duty, Simran gets to the surveillance before Arjun and thinks for a while.

What should I do first? Hmm...

When Arjun arrives, he was so surprised to see her there. He goes inside and stands next to her.

"Who fixed that?" he asked.

Shameless...just give me another taunt and you are done for!

"Oh you shouldn't care, idiot!" she replied, coolly.

"Come on! I'm seriously asking!"

"I'd rather take another hit than even talk to you."

"But you are, aren't you?"

"Yeah! I have no choice."

"You do. You can change your post..." he says.

Here's his plan!

"In that case, I'll be happy enough to talk to you." She says.

"But you can change it, you know!" he said.

"I'll take my chances! I've told you! I don't have anyone who cares about me!" she said and winked.

She winked at me!

Meanwhile, a letter comes to Aparna in the mailroom.

"From the…HQ?" she wondered and opened the letter. She read the letter andwas in shock.

Oh My God!

Suddenly Rishi entered and by seeing him she immediately hides the letter behind her back.

"What happened?" he asked.

"Nothing! Why are you here?" she asked, while crumpling the letter.

"I just passed by" – he saw the letter – "What's the letter?" he asked.

"It's...private! From my brother! And don't expect me to tell you everything just because you defend me!" she said and left.

Back to the surveillance room, Arjun was sitting in a corner trying to hatch up a plan but Simran was a step ahead of him. She moves closer to him. He felt weird and moved away. She moved closer and he moved away again. She edged closer again and he stopped.

What the hell?! What's she Doing?!

"Why do you have to come closer?!" he asked, getting angry and moving away.

"It's fun! To watch you feel so" – she moved closer – "awkward!" she said, and smirked.

She suddenly caught sight of his ring on his right hand. She grabbed hold of his hand and quickly took it off.

"Hey! Give that back!" he said, trying to grab it.

She rushed out of the room and went to the compound wall then threw it outside. It was long gone now. She went back inside.

"My uncle gave me that!" he said, angrily coming after her.

"It's good I threw it then. Your uncle wouldn't like this use of his ring!" she said, pointing to her jaw revealing a scratch.

He looked at his right hand and remembered.

"He gave it for protection..." he said.

Ugh. That must have hurt!

"Protection, huh! So you're afraid of me! I should have done the same but I'm not like you!" she said and smirked.

"Your weird! And happy!" he said and was walking away when he stopped at what Simran said.

"Many people say you keep your friends close but your enemies closer..." she said, while sitting on a chair.

Two can play at this game! Time to annoy her to get her out!

He thought and then he went and sat down in front of her.

"So if I'm your enemy...how close am I allowed to get?" he asked, while touching her hand and grabbing it tightly.

Immediately she grabs his other hand tightly.

"Is this one of your plans? Because if it is then I'm waiting for another hit!" she said.

They keep staring at each other.

"By the way!" said Simran and they break their stare.

"What?" he asked.

She goes close to him and so did he.

What's she doing now?

She stops just an inch away and grabs his hand then slams a file on it.

"What's this?" he asked.

"Indira gave responsibility of this file to be submitted to Princi by you! You have to write the explanation of the rubber bullets and blood in the ground and why were they found this way! Enjoy!" said Simran.

Damn her!

He grasped it, left and sat down on a chair next to her and started looking at the file in annoyance.

Chapter Thirteen – Not Again!

The next day, Aparna goes to school thinking.

Impossible! Raj was like this! Why me? I'll go to jail for no reason?! Not again! I haven't even done anything wrong this time! This is crap!

She tore the letter up and threw it in her room trashcan before going to school.

In break time, Rishi explains to Neerav what had happened and Neerav tells Shreya.

"Please do something!" he said.

"Why should I do it?" she asked.

"I don't know! For both of them?" he asked.

"No! I don't want to involve!" she said.

"Come on! Please!?" he asked.

"Please for what?" she asked.

"For looking for that letter!" he said, moving closer.

"Ok, fine! I'll do it! I'll do it! Stop it! Stop it!" she said, and pushed him away.

"Thank you!" he said and left.

In the evening, just before duty and after Aparna left her room, Shreya goes inside and starts rummaging for the letter and finally found it in two or three pieces in the trashcan. She takes out the pieces, tapes them together and reads it. This is the letter.

AGENT Aparna Deshpande
LOCKER 01

Anonymous has filed a case against you stating for murder. Until proven innocent you are hereby temporarily suspended from your post of duty at LOCKER 01 and will stay on leave.

Details located in official IB website.

AGENT Roy

IB Director General

HQ

"What! This is so bad!" said Shreya, in shock.

The next day, Shreya hands over the letter to Neerav in break time.

"Thanks! You're the best!" he said.

"I just did it for you! Nothing more!" she said.

"Still I owe you one!"

"I don't need anything! The letter is pretty bad!"

"Why do you have to show so much attitude?" he asked.

"I'm not! See you later!" she said and left.

Simran and Gaurav came and sat down.

"What's up?" she asked.

"A lot. You tell first." he said.

She narrated her incident in the surveillance room yesterday night.

"Oh god! What are you Doing?" he asked.

"Apparently a lot!" she said.

"I really under estimated you!" said Neerav.

"Yeah! That keeps happening!" she said.

"I thought you would get another hit from him but you're at least fine. Maybe he lightened up because your hit still isn't better and so was his." Said Neerav.

"Yeah! Plus you threw that ring of his away! Awesome!" said Gaurav.

"Yeah!" Neerav said.

"Your turn." She said.

He explains the letter and Simran reads it.

"This is too bad." she said.

"I know. Maybe Rishi will know how to deal with this!" Neerav said.

"Maybe Princi will know." Gaurav said.

"Let's see what to do later!" he said.

"So see you later on!" she said and left with Gaurav.

While walking,

"Arjun didn't leave his past?" asked Gaurav.

"He didn't! On the orientation class day I heard ma'am and Arjun talking. She was warning him of his past and to stay away from it." Said Simran.

"Looks like he didn't. What else did she say to him then, if you don't mind telling?" he asked.

"She said that he had health issues!" said Simran.

"I did hear Aakash making fun of him for that. He got pissed. Health issues...he seems fine to me." Said Gaurav.

"I know." Said Simran.

At lunch, Neerav tells everything to Rishi and even shows him the letter.

"Listen…you handle her and I think that the princi already knows so tell her that she will have to handle that too. Ok?" he said.

"All right. See you later, Neerav!" said Rishi and left.

At night duty, in the surveillance room Simran gets a thought and asks Arjun.

"So if a case is filed against somebody for murder in the IB court, then what will happen?" she asks.

"Why do you have to know?" he asks.

"I don't see your concern with it!"

"Seriously! How angry will you get?"

"Okay…forget that question."

"Why?" he asked.

"I need to go." She said, left the surveillance room and was going towards the inner gate when he stopped her in the corridor.

"Woah, what suddenly happened, miss know it all!? You can't take being with me in the surveillance?" he asked.

"Yeah! I just can't stay in the same place." She said.

"Then why don't you change your place?"

"No! That- I can't do that!"

"And why can't you do that?"

"I can't do it! I won't do it! You always do this! Kick out whomever you want from there. Believe me! I'll take another hit!"

"Why can't you just get lost from the surveillance?!" he said.

"No I'm not going to! I'm ready to adjust since we are partners!" she said.

"I will not! Just go from the surveillance!" he said.

"Do what you want but I'm not going anywhere!" she said.

"Such a girl! Always so much bothersome!" he said.

"You guys definitely misuse your power! Showing your pathetic temperament! That's not going to work on me!" she said.

That does it!

He grabs her hand when she struggled to go. She pushes him away and he leaves her hand hitting a wall. He comes to get her again when she punches him on his other jaw and kicks him again making him fall. He gets up.

Ah! That's even more painful! She's tough!

"I hate Doing that!" she said.

"Why do you do it?" he asked, aggressively.

"You don't listen!" she said.

He hits on her other jaw but she didn't fall. He kicks her and she fell on her knees. She gets up but she's still wobbly.

Please to my body. Don't fall now! I'm not done with him yet!

"Do you actually listen?!" he shouted.

"Oh no!" – the duty bell had rung and Simran was about to collapse when Arjun catches her and she pulls herself up – "The rest are going to be here and if they see this then they will kill you! Damn, I hate you!" she said, as she feels her jaw with blood again and he lets go of her.

Why is he catching hold of me? My stomach hurts! Ah!

"Okay! Here's a deal! We don't fight now! Come to the meeting room in five minutes and I'll meet you there with a first aid kit. Ok?" he said.

"Fine!" she said.

"You want some support or your good?" he asked.

"I said I'm fine!" she said and they both split up.

She's so cranky!

In five minutes Simran goes inside the LOCKER meeting room and closes the door. Arjun comes and closes the door later when he arrived.

"I'll fix yours first!" he said as he started to dress the wound.

"I don't need your help! Just do your own and leave me be!" she said and was going to leave when he stops her.

"You can't go to the infirmary with that. You might as well let me fix it!" he said.

She came back and sat down.

"Do your own. I'm just going to sit here then I'll go after everybody's asleep." She said.

He pushed her hair behind her and started to dab the wound with one hand and holding her face with another. She sighed.

"Is this also part of your plan?" she asked.

"Do me a favour and don't black out!"

"I have my doubts on whether you will hold onto your pain for that long!"

"Where the hell did you come from?"

"As if you're so interested!"

"Just tell…"

"You don't have to know! I'm not saying anything to you!"

"We might as well talk. It helps with the pain."

"I'm from Delhi…"

"I'm from Chandigarh... almost done." he said as he put on the bandage.

"Punjabi, huh." She said.

Not to be racist but that kind of explains a lot!

"I'm done! Your turn!"

He sits on the table while she stands and dresses his wound with one hand and holding his chin up with another.

"Ah! It hurts!"

"That's good to know! You actually feel pain!"

"Damn you! You successfully taunt me but I'm fighting the urge to punch you!"

"I certainly won't do it now because it's hard to put this stuff on you!"

"I haven't gotten worse from last time!"

"I know..."

They keep talking.

Meanwhile, Neerav wonders where they both were and checks the building and corridors. Back to the meeting room,

"Do you have a health problem?" asked Simran.

"No, what's making you ask that?" he asked.

"Aakash and you fought after the cricket tournament. It was about your health issue and Indu!" she said.

"I have nothing serious. I'm just a little lazy so I gym! And Indu was annoying me." he said.

"Fine, but if you pull Indu's hair one more time, I'll pull yours. If I don't, Aakash will." She said.

"Why do you have so many guns but never use them?" he asked, changing the topic.

"None of your business!" she said.

Just then, Neerav came inside after searching the entire school.

"Who did this?!" he said, as he came in.

"We did…" said Arjun.

"Yeah…" said Simran.

"Go out or something! You both do have a lot in common but you're just wasting your strength in hating each other. Try out something for once, Arjun!" said Neerav.

"Go out?" they both asked.

"Yeah! In fact, you both should stay here! It's Sunday tomorrow. Spend the night here! You both are too beaten up and everybody will start questioning anyway!" he said.

"Stay here…with him?" she asked.

"With her? No chance!" he said.

"You both are going to stay here. I'll see you both tomorrow morning and hopefully you won't kill each other till then!" Neerav said.

"Neerav! I didn't even eat anything!" said Simran.

"Yeah, me too! I'm starving!" said Arjun.

"Shut up and stay here!" said Neerav.

After saying that, he went outside and closed the room door then went and bolted the basement corridor door from outside. They were left locked in the corridor with only the LOCKER and the meeting room. They opened the door and saw the main corridor door locked.

"No use of trying! I'm done anyway!" said Simran, while keeping the box back in a drawer.

"Why? Can't you break it open?" he asked.

"Do you realize how hard that was?! My arms are still bruised and I got so many splinters from the nails in that old door!" she said.

"I told you to stay in there for your own good." He said.

"Don't you dare say that. If I hadn't called everybody and the cops down to the ground, you would've been dead. Just accept the fact that I saved your life and the LOCKER!" she said.

"Whatever...I'm tired, anyway...I'm going to sleep." He said.

"I'll sleep on the ground or something." Said Simran.

"You are as much hurt as I am so get up here!" he said.

"I'm serious. I feel more comfortable on the floor!" she said.

She lies down on the floor. He gets down and pushed the table to a side.

"Move over!" he said.

"No, just go!" she said.

"Why? Scared I'll do something to you? Or vice versa?" he said.

She scoffs and moves to her left. He lies down next to her.

"You're seriously a girl?" he asked.

"I swear, I'll kick you this time!" she said.

"I just haven't seen anyone like you!" he said.

She didn't reply.

So have I, Arjun! So have I!

"Anything else, miss know it all?" he asked.

"I wonder if Riya tried making out with you again." she said.

"Disgusting being that close to a girl like her." He said.

"And yet you are lying down just 5 centimetres away from me. Not disgusted?" she asked.

"I'm actually quite comfortable." He said.

Because she's hot…

"Now I feel disgusted!" she said.

But he's kind of cute…no! I'm still disgusted!

"Your seriously okay, right?" he asked.

"Stop asking! I'm a person, not a puppy! Let me sleep!" she said.

"Fine…" he said.

She murmured to herself "Idiot…"

Chapter Fourteen – The election.

The next day, in the early morning, Neerav arrived and opened the gate to see that Simran was awake and she gets down the table leaving Arjun, sleeping.

"Nice sleep…you both look great together!" said Neerav.

"Never again!" she said.

"This is a pretty good idea. I'll do this again if you two beat up each other!" he said.

"Oh you don't start getting any ideas! I can't stay in a place with him again! Did you get that?" she whispered so that Arjun wouldn't wake up.

"Are you afraid if he would wake up?" he asked.

"No! He's just better when he's asleep! See you later! Tell him that I'll see him in surveillance! We have to talk! I'm going to go eat!" she said and left.

Neerav woke him up.

"So I thought that I was crazy in having a dream like this but I'm not!" said Arjun.

"Shut up! It's real!" he said.

"That's the first time I've been that close to a girl and it didn't hurt, huh!" said Arjun, while rubbing his face.

"You both actually didn't beat the hell out of each other!" said Neerav.

"Yeah! We…uh…talked!"

"Talked?"

"Yeah…where did she go anyway?"

"I don't think you care, anyway!"

"Just tell me where she is! I need to talk to her!"

"She said that she'll see you in surveillance! That she wants to talk as well!"

"Oh!" he said.

"She said that she'll see you later too!" said Neerav and left.

Aparna, in the meantime, was brooding when Rishi comes.

"What do you want, Rishi?" she asked.

"Just to know one thing…what was in that letter?" he asked.

"I've already told you! It's personal!"

"Tell me!"

"You can't help me anyway!"

"It's a misunderstanding so don't worry!"

"Yeah…I know! I don't like it!"

Dude, you don't know everything! On what happened before that letter!

"So do I but it happens! And I don't like it either!" he said.

"I know that. Why do you have to be so worried about this?" she asked.

Let's take a break for a while and head over to what the Principal is Doing out of town.

Elsewhere, in New Delhi, at the IB HQ, in the conference debate hall all of the agents were assembled for results of the Directorial post.

"This was the ending of the last debate of the elections for the Director of the entire LSS branch!" said the announcer. The audience scoff.

"Anyway" – he continued- "we have narrowed down to only two contestants: Agent Varun Srinivas and Agent Vijayanti Rao. After a totalling of the votes we have a winner!" he said. Someone comes from backstage and gives a card to the announcer.

"Sorry...just had the card changed. Now our winner is… Agent Varun Srinivas!" said the announcer.

Everybody claps.

Later, after the assemble, the Principal(Vijayanti Rao) goes in the lift downwards when it stops at the twelfth floor(total 20 floors and the debate conference hall was on the 15th floor). The Director's secretary gets in the lift and it closes.

"So...I'm sorry!" said the secretary.

I'm chairperson of the LSS committee! He's less capable than me! I've never even seen him at any committee meeting of any sort! How dare they choose him!

"I know that! Even I wanted to work with you!" replied the Principal. "I'm sure that you'll have a good time!"

"You're not serious, right?"

"Of course, not! He cheated anyway!"

"I realized that when they got the card changed on the spot!"

"I had suspicions before because he was quite close to the ex Director!"

"Everybody's so bad!"

"I know! That's why I'm really pissed! Corrupt people!"

"Cool down, Vijayanti! Ok?"

"Yeah! But we're going to figure out a way! Don't we always?" said the Principal.

The lift opens at the ground floor. They step out and start walking towards the airbase.

"Anyway...bye for now!" said the Principal.

"By the way, Varun filed a stupid case of murder on Agent Aparna Deshpande! And he used the ex Director for that!

I've cleared her name so she doesn't have anything to worry about! But..." said the secretary.

"But what?" asked the Principal.

"Her brother got justice…but he got killed by unknown shooters when he attempted to escape!" said the secretary.

"Well, she has to know! She can handle pain! Thanks for clearing her name!" said the Principal.

"I got plane tickets for Varun so that he will be at Jammu and Kashmir for a while and I'm going to fix as much as I can!" she said.

"Okay. Anything else?" asked the Principal.

"Is it true? That robbery attempt on LOCKER 01? Is that true?" she asked.

"Well, I am in charge of safe guarding a LOCKER. So robbery attempts can definitely be made!" said the Principal.

"I'm serious. That was a professional team and they've been preparing to rob LOCKER 01 for two months. They even sent an undercover guy to scan the entire premises. How was that stopped?" she asked.

"I had a great army base nearby. They were on alert!" said the Principal.

"I don't know how you do it. Your LOCKER is definitely the safest." She said.

"You know it is." She replied.

The bid each other and the secretary leaves. Just then a well known face came over to her. A well built, slightly tanned man having silky brown hair with a formal shirt and jeans having his sleeves rolled up. He came with a few files in one hand of his and they shook hands.

"I heard the news. It's pretty shocking. I barely know the guy." He said.

"It's okay, as long as no trouble is caused." She said.

"I barely see you here anymore, Agent Rao. Is the school being too tough to handle?" he asked.

"Not at all. The LSS agents on the other hand are a huge pain this year. They don't function together. Everybody has some problem and they can't get over it!" she said.

"You don't mean my daughter, do you?" he asked.

"Of course not, Agent Khanna! She and her friend are doing great! Everybody else is only the problem." She replied.

"Great! What about that robbery everybody's talking about? Something to be worried about?" he asked.

"Well, nothing was taken. And the police arrived just in time. I was surprised when my assistant told me that some agent wounded a few of them alone. They couldn't move! But what about the interrogation?" she asked.

"The leader is very wanted. His team was training with him for two years. And he wasn't saying anything. One panic stricken member was. Courtesy of me." He said.

"Your still good even with a desk job." She said.

"That's good...good to know." He said.

"What's wrong? Any problem?" she asked.

"No, it's just family matters. Nothing serious!" he said.

"Okay...if you say so!" she said.

"Anyway, I have work now so just tell her to be careful. And Agent Chopra should not hit anybody. Heh, heh. Okay, see you soon." He said.

"Bye!" she said.

He turns around and leaves and she goes in the opposite direction. Then the Principal goes to the helipad and leaves in her chopper.

In the evening, in the surveillance room, Arjun and Simran talk.

"So what did you want to talk about?" asked Simran.

"About yesterday…" he started.

"It never happened! I know!"

"Not exactly that!"

"Then what?"

"I mean, it got me thinking!"

"That you should look for better methods to get rid of me?"

"I swear, I'm not that bad as you think!"

"How am I supposed to believe that when you keep on faking your apologies?!"

"Oh come on! It was only one time! Get over it!"

"Okay! Anyway, it really doesn't matter because you won!"

"What do you mean?"

"Surveillance is all yours. I talked to Princi! She wanted to talk to you!"

"Wait! You're leaving?"

"Yes, bye!"

"Wait!"

"I don't want to talk to you anymore! So please just leave me be!"

"But-" he started.

"Just please DON'T talk to me!" she snapped.

He stayed silent. She then left.

Wow! That...was unexpected.

They notice a car arrive at the North gate. Radhika contacts Arjun.

"Who is it?" he asked.

"Princi...she's back and we are going to have to meet her tomorrow! But she wants to see you in her cabin before night duty!" said Radhika.

"Cool!" said Arjun.

Why now?

Natasha was going to duty when she saw Simran in the storeroom. She looked closer to see that she was sitting on an old bench with a tablet in one hand and a wrench in another. She also had grease marks on her face. A hover board was dismantled next to her. Natasha came in and stood in front of her.

What is she doing?!

"What are you doing here? You should be at duty!" she said. "Apparently the Principal might change my post from the surveillance! So I'm just fixing this hover board. I should do something!" said Simran.
"Scared of Arjun? It's about time!" said Natasha.

Yeah, think whatever you want. I'm going anyway!

Simran didn't say anything and continued to work on the hover board.
"That's useless! You can't possibly know about the parts of that thing to fix it. The battery is dead and dirty!" she said.

"No, the chemical to power up the battery is not able to go in, so the pipe is clogged. I cleaned it and it will work!" said Simran, while attaching the last part on it.

"It won't work!" said Natasha.

Simran turned it on and it revved up just like new.

"Nothing is ever useless!" said Simran, getting up and grabbing the board after switching it off and her tablet. "Don't you have duty?"

"Yeah…" said Natasha and left.

At night duty, Radhika reached the north gate and saw Gaurav on his cell phone talking. He turned around and saw her and signaled her to keep quiet. She nodded.

"Yeah, mom!" he said.

"How can you just be mean to Aanya like that?! You know how good she is! You'll never get any girl! Her parents are our friends!" she scolded.

"She is so clingy! Admit it! You just want some guarantee girl for me, don't you? What? Think that I can't get married later?" he asked.

"I know that you won't want marriage. I'm just planning your future for you! And this is what you do! Some night guard job! I swear, after this, I will make you get a degree and you will be thankful to have a real job and a family!" she said.

"Excuse me? I never asked you to be the boss of my future! After this, I'll get a very good job! With even better pay than yours!" he said.

"How dare you-" she started.

"No, that's it! I've had it with you! After school, I'm moving out! And I don't care about marriage! Don't call me to talk about these things!" he said, cut the call and threw the phone behind him but Radhika caught it.

"Can you afford a new phone if this breaks?" she asked, while giving it to him.

"Damn, sorry!" he said and took it.

"So you have problems with your parents!" she said.

"It's personal!" he said.

"I know, I'm just saying!" she said. "But they called you for Aanya?"

"Yeah, they think they can do anything. It's my life! I'm going to choose what will happen to me!" he said.

"Yeah, although don't start expecting that from now. We are still in school and we don't have jobs yet. So start being careful by taking care of your phone!" she said.

"Yeah...right!" he said. "Thanks!"

"No problem!" she said.

Chapter Fifteen –
Permanently Dismissed!

Arjun reached her cabin and waited outside. The peon called him in and he went inside. She came and stood in front of him.

"You defied me. And that robbery attempt could've blown your cover if Agent Khanna didn't act to the situation! Now you both have to go to Kashmir!" said the Principal.

"I didn't kick her out. She left herself!" he said.

"She left because you both fought! So I've had enough! You will be given orders-" she started.

"Ma'am, please! You can't send us there!" he said.

"I have no choice! I can't believe you!" she said.

"Please, ma'am! It won't happen again! I will get her back myself! I swear, I will!" he said and pleaded.

"Fine! But next time..." she said.

"It won't happen again! Thank you, ma'am!" he said and left hurriedly.

She let him go.

The next day, at lunchtime, everyone was standing outside of the Principal's office.

"Why did princi call us?" asked Indira, who couldn't stay quiet any longer.

"Do we know? No! And if we did then wouldn't we tell you?!" Priya replied.

"I wasn't even asking you!" snapped Indira.

"Shut Up! Both of you!" said Simran.

"Cool down! Just remember that when you want to ask something then first tell whom do you want the answer from!" said Priya, coolly.

"You are" started Indira.

"Shut Up, Indu!" – he pulls her hair and puts his finger on her mouth and smirks a bit – "Just for a little while! You'll get your answers!" said Aakash.

He's being nice to me! Again with the hair...

The rest give a few fake coughs and Indira moves his hand annoyingly. Nikhil noticed Natasha in deep thought.

"Hey, Natasha!" he whispered.

"What?" she asked.

"What's wrong? Anything happened?" he asked.

"No, nothing!" she said and continued thinking.

How did she fix that? That thing wasn't working for a year. It was just in that store room! She knows a lot!

After a few minutes, the Principal send for them. As they come in, they noticed that an army official was also present.

"Good Day, sir!" everyone saluted.

"Good Day…" he said.

"Well,…uh…yeah! I've been out of town. As the Director elections were being held" started the Principal but somebody interrupted her.

"She lost…and the new Director has issued a set of rules that have you all permanently dismissed from your duties. He has other things in mind for you all." Said the official.

Everybody was shocked.

"But sir! They can't do that!" spoke up Neerav.

"Your joking, right?" asked Arjun.

"I just got here! You can't do that!" protested Ankita.

"LISTEN!" shouted the Principal and everyone suddenly became silent.

"Please understand!" she said.

"We don't make the decisions here!" said the official.

"Yes! And Agent Pandey, mind your tongue!" said the Principal.

"Agent Deshpande's termination letter was also a fake! Agent Rao, I'll have to go now so we'll talk later!" said the official and he left.

"Listen carefully...he placed his own Agents here and right now just keep an eye on them. Surveillance, school and hostels can still need security. Is that clear?" instructed the Principal.

"Yes, ma'am!" they said.

"You may go now! But Agent Deshpande! Stay back please!" said the Principal.

The rest leave and Aparna has a word with the Principal then she comes back but goes to her hostel room and shuts the door.

Later, in the afternoon, everyone sits down on the stairs of the hostel entrance.

"How dare that Director!" said Radhika, getting really angry.

"I know! I mean, we all do!" said Raghav.

Simran pressed Radhika's shoulder slightly for calming her down.

"How can the Director do that?! He has no authority! Authority isn't even there for dismissing the top 400 agents and look at this!" said Indira.

"Who's the Director anyway?!" asked Aakash.

"What do we know?!" asked Neerav.

"Nobody knows..." said Nikhil.

"Yeah for his protection." Said Natasha.

"I feel like killing him. My job..." said Arjun.

Everybody kept on grumbling for a while.

"Does it matter?" asked Simran, speaking up while looking up from her phone.

Everyone stopped talking and looked at her bewildered.

"Does what matter?" asked Natasha.

"Does knowing the Director's name matter?" asked Simran, casually.

"Yeah!" said Shreya.

"What will you do if you know?" asked Simran, casually again.

"We can do quite a lot with a name. We can expose him." Said Aakash.

"That's out of the question." Said Gaurav.

"Yeah, exposing him will expose the LSS. Think properly!" said Radhika.

"His name is Varun Srinivas! Do what you want." said Simran.

Natasha immediately searches her tablet but doesn't find anything of him. Nikhil searches again and doesn't find it.

"It's not in here!" said Nikhil.

"Of course, it's not. You said yourself!" she said.

"Then how do you know?" asked Aakash.

"I have my ways." She said and went back to her phone.

"Let's see tomorrow!" said Arjun.

They all leave for duty.

But Arjun doesn't find Simran in the surveillance room. He goes out and looks for her.

In the ground, Simran was thinking,

I will be able to get it! I guess I will have to brush up a few things! But what about the transfer? Also, I had to leave that habit! Damn, the transfer! I feel like fixing another board. There were quite a lot in that room, just thrown away. Natasha caught me, though. Whatever, I will be transferred anyway! Oh, damn! That transfer! What was I thinking?!

Arjun noticed and went to her.

"Do you even realize what I had to do for you?!" he said.

"Do what?" she asked.

"I had to go beg Princi to not transfer us! Are you insane?! She warned me..." he started and told everything, while sitting down.

"I knew way before. I was willing to risk it." She said as he sat down next to her.

"Oh really!" – he puts his arm around her – "Tell me more!" he said.

She moves away.

"Hey! I'm not going to hurt you!" he said.

"Said the guy who torments everybody!" she said.

"I'm serious..." he said, slowly.

She comes back next to him and he puts his arm around her.

"Now, here's a deal. You will come back to the surveillance room with me and we're going to work something out. Okay?" he asked.

"No, okay? I've had enough of you! I really don't care about any Border Security Force anywhere!" she said.

"I do! I don't care but we can't handle them there. Just please, let's go for duty!" he said.

She was silent for a while.

Should I? We? He doesn't care about me! He just wants his ass off of trouble! But he's got a point! I can't handle the Border soldiers. They are horrid!

"We'll start tomorrow!" she said.

"Why?" he asked.

"I have file work!" she said.

"Okay..." he said.

"But we are just partners. Not friends!" she warned.

"I don't want to be friends with a crazy girl like you!" he said.

"As if I want to be friends with an asshole like you! No way!" she said and left.

The next day, everybody assembled in the meeting room which Simran had called. Radhika came early and they both talk.

"Why did you call the meeting? And who did this to your face?!" asked Radhika.

"I've done something that I thought I should have left the habit! And it's a long story so I'll tell you later!" replied Simran.

"You hacked who's PC?!"

"The Principal's…"

"You what?!"

"I told you! I was curious on this guy and I tried to find his file but my tablet wasn't having it! So princi's had a wider range of files so I looked in there and got this!"

"Oh my god! Do you realize how much trouble you could get in?! I thought you left that!"

"Oh come on! I know that even you wanted to!"

"Yeah! But I went at 1:00 and found princi's shadow typing!"

"What was the time?"

"1:00 am. Why?" she asked.

"I was hacking her tablet then!" said Simran.

They looked at each other for a minute and Radhika smacked her forehead and laughed. Everyone came inside and Simran shows a paper but before that.

"Where is Aparna?" asked Simran.

"Sick!" said Natasha.

"For two days?" asked Simran.

"Yeah!" she replied.

"So I have called because I wanted to ask you who this is?" asked Simran, while showing a picture of the Director.

"Varun Srinivas…are we missing something?" asked Priya.

"Yeah…" – she showed a photo – "Who's this?" asked Simran.

"Who?" asked Nikhil.

"Prakash Kapoor…" – she shows both of their pictures together – "anything?" asked Simran.

"This seems weird but their eyes are looking the same!" said Arjun.

"They don't look same! They are same!" she said.

"He's a criminal? Hey! I was joking before about checking for a file of his!" said Natasha.

Simran showed a criminal record.

IB

CRIMINAL RECORD NUMBER 1052

NAME – Prakash Kapoor

AGE – 25 years old

CRIMES – Murders, robberies, destroying of national artifacts and illegal arms businesses[Details in Archive records]

CASES – 2 for Murder, 7 robberies, destroyed article 17 from LOCKER 10.

PUNISHMENT GIVEN – 20 years at Tihar jail.

"So we should get a ID match?" asked Aanya.

"Where did you get this?" asked Arjun.

"I told you...I have my ways." said Simran and left.

I'm not about to answer him!

"Meeting over? Bye!" said Rishi and left.

Chapter Sixteen – Hackers…

In the evening, in the surveillance room, Arjun sees Simran bothered and puts his arm around her.

"What's bugging you, miss know it all? Seriously!" asked Arjun, while seeing his face in a cracked mirror at the corner.

Shit! I won't be able to hide this! At least nobody notices me anyway!

"You deactivate bombs! Were you trained for that? Or was it just a habit?" she asked.

"It was a habit but I trained more! Why? What's the matter?"

"Nothing…"

"You might as well tell!"

"I have a habit which I can't stop!"

"What?" – he takes off his hand from his jaw and sits down in front of her – "What habit?"

"I can access any computer, tablet and phone in the entire government defence system."

"What?"

"I'm a hacker…"

He was silent for just a moment. After coming to,

"Who else? Just you?"

"Me and Radhika…" she said.

"You are way more interesting than I've thought! That's how she won the quiz!" he said.

"Yeah…whatever!" said Simran, feeling her jaw.

"So that's your way!" he said.

"You tell anybody and you're dead!" she said.

My god! It's purple! It looks so obvious!

"Nobody will know! Stop touching that. You'll make it worse!" he said.

"It already is!" she said.

At the hostel room of Aparna and Natasha, in the meantime, Aparna was on her bed while Natasha was talking to her.

"You can't stay here forever! You need to get over this!" said Natasha.

"Raj is dead! Just because he didn't get his case solved in time!" said Aparna.

"I know your sad about your brother but please don't miss school or duty!"

"I can't face anybody right now!"

"Want me to get Rishi?"

"What am I going to even talk about if I see him?"

"Just talk! I'm going to get him tomorrow and you both will talk!" she said and left.

Radhika comes to the surveillance.

"Simran, we need to talk!" said Radhika.

"Is Raghav over there?" asked Arjun.

"Yeah! Simran, please!" said Radhika.

"Fine!" she said and they go outside then talk when Raghav goes in to talk to Arjun.

"Simran…who did that to your face?" she asked.

"I told you! It's nothing!" she replied.

"Come on! You're a bad liar! Did you and Arjun get into a fight?"

"Arjun?"

"I saw his face too! You beat him up pretty bad and so did he! He's the guy!?"

"Yeah, so?"

"What happened?"

"He locked me in the surveillance room once and so we got in a fight after that 'Brad' incident!"

"That looks like two days ago!" she said.

"He brought up that topic again! So we got in another fight!" said Simran.

Meanwhile, Raghav starts to interrogate Arjun.

"You beat up a girl?" said Raghav, trying to digest.

"Yeah…" said Arjun.

"And she beat you up more!"

"Yeah…"

"Your shameless… you know that, right?"

"Yeah…"

"Then again…she's as shameless as you are!"

"What?"

"You both do have a lot in common!"

"Why do you people keep saying that?! Stop it!" said Arjun.

"Okay! I'll see you later…" said Raghav and left with Radhika.

Simran comes back in and they had no more talking after that.

The next day, Radhika called a meeting. Gaurav came early to the meeting room.

"Uh… princi gave a notice…" she said.

"Ok… show!" he said.

She did and he was surprised.

"Are you sure?" he asked.

"Yeah!" she said

"You're lying to me! Where did you get this?!" he asked.

"I…found it…" said Radhika.

"This was erased, wasn't it?"

"Yeah…"

"Then how and where did you find it?"

"I found it in princi's tablet…"

"You're a hacker, aren't you?"

"How do you know?!"

"Simran…"

"Oh…you know quite a lot about us, huh."

"Yeah…"

"It's just a habit! Simran and I-"

"I know…"

"Yeah and it's just a habit so please don't freak out!"

"Okay…it's fine."

"So…"

"How are you going to tell where you got it?"

"I haven't thought about that! I wasn't going to tell!"

"How about you leave? I'll handle it! Don't let Simran come either!" he said.

"Okay!" she said.

She left and when everybody arrived,

"Where's Radhika?" asked Nikhil.

"She was called! Princi called her!" lied Gaurav.

"And where's Aparna and Simran?" asked Priya.

"Aparna's still sick!" said Natasha.

Everybody looked at Arjun.

"What? Why are you looking at me?" asked Arjun, while keeping his head turned at an angle.

"She's your partner!" saidAakash.

"I don't know, okay? She maybe running late!" he said with his head still turned.

"And Rishi?" asked Aanya.

"I don't know about that! I just wanted to show this!" said Gaurav and showed a paper.

IB

NOTICE 1174

Candidates of election of 2015 for post of Director

First position: AGENT Varun Srinivas

Runner up: AGENT Vijayanti Rao

"I don't understand! We know this!" said Siddharth.

"This was erased!" said Aakash.

"Then where did you find it?" asked Raghav.

"First we should think about the cause on why it was erased and by whom!" said Arjun, saving Gaurav.

Everyone turned around but Arjun casually put his hand under his chin to cover his purple jaw.

He's covering for me! He's covering his jaw too. They will ask when they find out.

"Well, someone erased it so quickly!" said Shreya.

"Without any authorized procedure…" said Neerav.

"This leads to the Director! I'm sure!" said Natasha.

"He got this done! Only a third party can do this!" said Aneesh.

"Which brings us back to the question of where did you find it?" asked Ankita.

Arjun and Gaurav looked at each other then shrugged at them.

"YOU both are definitely hiding something!" said Nikhil.

"No..." said Simran, while coming in with a scarf around her neck to cover her jaw.

Everyone looked at her.

"There is something wrong with you! It's hot today! What's with the scarf?" asked Priya.

"Oh, like I'm going to tell you!" said Simran.

She glared at her then looked away in ignorance.

"Yeah, what are you hiding under there?" asked Raghav.

Don't do it! What are you going to say? We may get sent to Kashmir!

She takes off her scarf and puts it on the table.

"Happy now?" asked Simran, with sarcasm.

Shreya goes and pulls up her chin and is shocked to see a bruise there. Everybody is. Arjun gets up as well and everybody sees him too wide eyed. Nikhil goes to him and touches his bruise.

"Stop it, it still hurts!" said Arjun.

"Explain this! Now!" said Nikhil.

"I will not!" he said.

"We are diverting here!" said Siddharth.

"Just wait a second! Explain now!" said Nikhil. "Did you two fight?"

"Yeah..." said Simran.

"Why?" asked Nikhil.

Neither of them answered and just looked at each other.

"Answer me!" said Nikhil.

Everyone looked at her.

What do I say? Come on! Think!

"He insulted my mother!" lied Simran.

Everybody then looked at Arjun.

Mother?! She did pass away...come on! I can say something!

"She died anyway, what does it matter?!" said Arjun, going along with her.

"Don't make me hit you again!" shouted Simran.

"Oh, I'm ready to take you on again! Come on!" said Arjun, taunting her.

She was about to go to punch him when Radhika and Shreya pulled her back.

Nikhil pulled back Arjun.

All this time Natasha was thinking.

Those two...they know quite a lot...Simran got that criminal record...it's impossible to get it...Radhika could answer that question about the wires so easily...she knows so much...she must have recovered that notice...also they must have erased everything about themselves! I keep seeing Simran on some gadget. She could fix that hover board!

"Hackers...you both are hackers!" said Natasha, after realising.

"That's illegal!" said Siddharth.

"Who are you to tell her that?!" said Radhika just entering.

"Yeah, from what I know, most of you are from top training camps where they already gave you orientation classes! Nikhil and Natasha, your test wasn't rigged but you received illegal training before joining for training." said Simran.

"You both are taking classified information!" said Priya.

"So are you! So shut up!" said Indira, defending Simran.

Radhika grabs a laptop and puts a scanner in it. Simran scans the election results and the criminal record with it. Radhika enters a few codes and starts an identity match. It took a minute or two to load and it showed the two pictures of now and before saying "ID Perfect Match".

Simran starts typing codes and searches for the IP address of the hacker who erased the documents. After typing a few codes it starts loading.

"Remember what was the logo drawn on the brick in which the bomb was kept?" she asked.

"Kapoor Enterprise! Fancy writing with a couple of stars. Why?" asked Nikhil.

It finished loading.

"A hacker from there erased this! I got it's IP address too but" said Simran and stopped when she noticed the screen turning black for a moment.

"What? Where is it?" asked Raghav.

"Oh no…shit…" said Radhika and shut down the laptop.

"What happened?" asked Indira.

Simran and Radhika glanced at each other and then to them.

Simran took out her gun and gave it to Radhika who immediately shot four times on the laptop and it was destroyed!

Chapter Seventeen – Caught!

"Why did you guys do that?!" said Gaurav.

"We are so stupid, Radhika!" said Simran.

"Now what are we going to do?! We're dead!" said Radhika.

"Excuse me! But explain!" said Arjun.

"Somebody was spying on us through that laptop!" said Simran.

"That's why you shot it!" said Aakash.

"How did you get real bullets?" asked Priya.

"I..." Simran started.

"I got them for her. I have my methods!" said Arjun, saving her.

He's covering for me! Why?

They were surprised.

Meanwhile, Rishi goes to the hostels when he hears someone crying. He goes and sees that Aparna was crying. He opened the doors and sees her crouched on the floor.

"What happened?!" asked Rishi.

"Just…leave!" said Aparna.

"No! Get up!" – he grabs her hand and pulls her up then he makes her sit on her bed – "So first…stop crying!" he said and wiped her tears.

"Would you leave?!!?" she shouted.

"I can't do that!" – he sits down next to her – "Why are you crying?! Your safe, right?" he asked.

She tells everything which happened with the principal.

"Now he's gone!" she said.

"I'm sorry…I guess I should go!" he said and made his way for the door.

"It's not your fault!" she said and he stopped.

"I know! So you can have your privacy!" he said.

"I have to tell you something!" she started and he cut her off.

"Okay, what?" he asked.

"I was in jail before. Just two years. It was because of blowing my parents' cover. After that brutal juvenile, I've just been worried all the time! I'm just saying this so that you stop defending me. I can take care of myself! Okay?" she said.

"Sure!" – he turns around then goes and sits down with her – "I'm fine with it! But I never knew you were jail material!" he said.

"What?" she asked.

Back to the situation in the meeting room.

"You guys…" started Ankita.

"You'll kill us, you know that?" said Siddharth.

"Yeah! Plus, even if ma'am doesn't know, she'll enquire about that laptop! Shit." said Neerav.

"But now it's done, Prakash knows where she is!" said Radhika.

"What?" a few were confused.

"Don't you know? The Director does not know where agents are placed. Only a few administrative people know." Said Nikhil.

"Sorry!" said Simran.

"Don't be! We're in this together!" said Natasha.

"Seriously?" asked Arjun.

"Yeah, we're a team, deal with it!" said Natasha.

Really?! She's saying that?!

Back to the hostels, Aparna and Rishi were still talking.

"Your amusing, right?" asked Aparna.

"I'm serious! I'm not a good agent!" said Rishi.

"You're a great agent!"

"Why do you think that?!"

"I know! Ask anybody!"

"No!"

"Okay...tell me one thing!"

"Sure!"

"Why do you keep defending me?"

"I can't say that!"

"Say! It's only me!"

"I guess I just like you!"

"Oh wow! That's sweet!"

"Oh..."

"I have a thing for you too! Just a thing, though!" she said.

"Really?" he asked.

The next day, in the break time, everyone was standing outside the Principal's office.

"You think she called for..." said Indira.

"Indu, even I don't know!" asked Priya.

She's not insulting me, weird!

"Hmm..." said Priya.

Arjun was standing next to Raghav and Simran. He noticed her trying different hand positions to cover her bruise.

"What's wrong?" he whispered to her.

"Your bruise looks even more obvious today! And so does mine!" said Simran.

"She won't ask anything! It shouldn't matter to her!" he said.

"She's going to kill me..." said Simran.

She's going to do that then tell my dad! Damn!

The Principal's assistant comes out and calls them. They go inside and stand.

"Good-" they started but she cut them off.

"Agent Singh! What happened to your face?" she asked.

"Nothing! I fixed it anyway!" he said, defending himself.

"Fine! Simran-I mean, Agent Khanna? Why do you look as beat up as him?" she asked.

"Nothing! It's fine, anyway!" said Simran.

"Coming back! I want to know who hacked into some information from my personal tablet!" she shouted.

Nobody said anything. Not a single word.

"Listen! If you don't step forward then I will transfer all of you..." said the Principal.

Immediately Simran and Radhika stepped forward.

"Good! Except both of you, the rest may wait outside. Now!" she said.

They all go and stand outside.

In her office,

"I need you to hack this old tablet and bring back some erased data!" she said.

"What?" they both were astonished.

"The Director threw it and a friend of mine had found it! You should be looking for a few newspaper articles having arrests of him before and it has uplinks with his company partners like e mails and video chats! Start with the password!" she said and they both started quickly as if they had a gun pointed on their heads.

"Okay...I need that scanner from my room! Radhika, just run over and get it!" said Simran while entering codes.

"Sure!" she said and goes out to get it.

Everybody sees her going and were confused.

"I'm surprised she's not dead yet. She looks busy!" said Natasha.

"I hope you learned that they are as good as we are! Maybe even better! You should expand your mind!" said Nikhil.

"They just beat me in my favourite things..." she said.

"Your good enough!" he said.

"I saw Simran once in the store room before going for duty." She said.

"Store room? What was she doing there?" he asked.

"She fixed a hover board that was broken down for a year! It works like new now!" she said.

"She did? Wow. I have to see that!" he said.

"Yeah, aren't you impressed! She proved me wrong and you are just impressed at her!" she said.

"Don't act proud, Natasha. Hackers can fix any machine. They even know all parts in a machine! They are geniuses. It's the first time I saw another one!" he said.

"How do you know?" she asked.

"You can't win over a hacker. My dad was one!" he said.

"Really? What exactly does he do?" she asked.

"He fixes broken weapons in defence! Sometimes he is called to fix aircraft or review missiles!" he said.

"You never told me that before!" she said.

"That's because you never asked!" he said.

Meanwhile, Arjun was worried as he saw Radhika go back in.

"What's going to happen to Simran?" whispered Arjun to Gaurav.

"Your caring for your enemy!" whispered back Gaurav.

"Shut up, I don't!" he said.

In the Principal's office, they both were finished.

"Your good! Better than I've expected!" said the Principal.

"You're not going to do anything to us, right?" asked Simran.

"No! Your too valuable to transfer! But don't tell the rest of them that!" she said.

"Oh thank god!" said Radhika.

Suddenly the phone rings and the Principal puts it on speaker.

"Hey! It's me! Diana!" said the Director's secretary on the other line.

"Good! I have two agents/hackers who helped me get a few things. Agent Simran Khanna and Agent Radhika Chopra!" said the Principal.

"They are top 400...what did they do?" she asked.

"They are top 50 actually. Simran, she's the daughter of Agent Khanna!" said the Principal.

"She topped the test, right?" she said.

"Yes, working hard on her own!" said the Principal.

"Wait, you know that Nikhil and Natasha..." said Simran.

"All too well. But they are still fine. I don't expect anything from them but I expect a lot of good things from you! Remember that!" she said.

"Yes, ma'am!" she said.

"Oh wow! She's that good, huh...anyway, the Director's back! I couldn't do so much!" said Diana.

"It's okay! It happens!" said Ajay, the Principal's assistant.

"I'm annoyed with him! A fellow with no respect!" she said.

"That he is!" said the Principal.

"He looks kind of familiar!" said Diana.

"Yeah, because of this!" said Radhika and she showed the criminal record.

"Prakash Kapoor...your father and I worked with him." said the Principal.

"So he was an agent of your post." Said Simran.

"Yeah when we were 23. He was arrested after two years. Looks like he knows where I'm posted. " Said the Principal.

"Yeah, sorry!" said Radhika.

"Anything else?" asked Diana.

"Search for 'Kapoor Enterprise' once!" said Simran.

"A minute…" – she puts the phone on the table and types something in the computer next to her – "It's an arms supplier for terrorists! Accused in breaking prison walls to free prisoners." said Diana.

"Oh my god!" said the Principal.

She sends for the rest of the agents and they come inside.

"We're all on the same side! You hate the Director and so do we." Started the Principal.

"We have to work together and we have someone to help us! She is Diana, the Director's secretary!" said Ajay, the Principal's assistant.

"Kapoor Enterprise is the business that he started." said the Principal.

"After rehabilitating him we let him go! But I guess the memory eraser didn't work so he got a plastic surgery done! Only his eyes are the same but he's a different person!" explained Ajay.

Everybody was bewildered.

"He's got a different motive!" said Nikhil.

"He works under no politician!" said Natasha.

"We'll have to get it out from him!" said Ajay.

"I have an idea!" said the Principal, smirking.

"What?" everyone asked.

"It'll take some time and discussing it here is not safe! You're all relieved from duty and the day after tomorrow I want all of you in uniform at 7:00AM." said the Principal.

"It's going to take some time for me to take a day off but I will try!" said Diana and cut the phone.

"Board the bus in uniform! We have to go to my research lab! You may go!" said the Principal and they left.

Outside when everybody leaves, Radhika and Simran come out last.

Chapter Eighteen – In Danger!

When going in a corridor upstairs in the main building, Simran and Radhika noticed one of the Director's team of Agents nearing the surveillance room.

"Saw that?" asked Simran.

"You bet I did. Let's go!" said Radhika.

He enters the surveillance room and they immediately go in after him. Simran went in and shut the door while taking out her gun and Radhika stood guard outside.

"Stop right there!" she said.

"Agent Khanna! I've heard a lot about you! Especially that you can't shoot anybody! I keep wondering why. Your dad is good and so is your older brother! He's an expert!" he said.

"I can shoot. I'm the best in the top 400 and top 50. Surely better than you! I just choose not to show it, you know!" she said.

"Yeah, you're afraid to be like him. You know who I'm talking about!" he said.

"I'm not afraid of anything. I would love to kill you if you don't tell me what you are Doing here! You are not authorised to be here!" she said.

"Whatever. You will go somewhere else anyway. The boss certainly wants to kill you and your father!" he said.

"You certainly read up on me!" – while clicking her gun – "You shouldn't have. Now I can kill you so easily!" she said.

"You never killed anyone before. You certainly can't kill me!" he said.

"Your right!" – shooting his thigh and he falls – "I can shoot you, though!" she said while still pointing her gun.

"Damn you!" he said.

"Get up. I don't want your blood here. Terrace. Now!" she said and he obeyed.

While going back to class,

"What do you think?" asked Nikhil.

"I don't know! He's a very confusing criminal!" said Natasha.

"Maybe he has a personal motive!" said Nikhil.

"I don't know…" she said.

"And yet again, Simran didn't say anything until we almost got in trouble!" he said.

"Anyway, it isn't safe for us to talk about this anymore so I'll see you later!" said Natasha.

"Bye!" said Nikhil and left.

She left.

Nikhil goes to the library after classes and when he reaches the back shelf, Arjun falls at his feet saying "You've got to help me!"

He immediately tells something in his ear.

"The nearby town?" asked Nikhil.

"Yeah! Please!" said Arjun.

"You think that they would have any info on him?" asked Nikhil.

"They should. The said that where you have to go is most safe and they don't want any chances by meeting me! Okay?" said Arjun.

Arjun couldn't go meet any accomplices. First of all, he was supposed to get rid of them because it wasn't in the IB policy. Also, if they were caught meeting each other then it would be too risky.

"Okay! I got it!" said Nikhil.

After a while, Nikhil was on his way to the hostels. Natasha was talking to Shreya and Indira.

"What's the chemistry with Nikhil? It's still there, huh!" asked Shreya.

"Why are you saying that? It's" – spots Nikhil – "nothing like that at all" said Natasha.

"Something is there! Whenever you see him you'll stop like that and then you'll make an excuse and, I don't know, go talk to him? Nat? Are you even listening to me?" said Indira.

She so wants him back!

"Oh! There he is! Natasha!!" said Shreya.

"What!?" said Natasha, startling.

"I've heard that Aparna's brother, I mean, another brother of hers was in contact with Prakash! They are a trio!" said Shreya.

"Still in contact?" asked Natasha.

"No! They traded a few business of arms but no more!" said Indira.

"Oh!" said Natasha.

Simran, Radhika and the Agent reach the terrace of the hostels since everybody was at school. At one push, the agent falls down in pain with the bullet still in his thigh.

"How do you know about me?" she asked.

"I'm paid to kill you by the boss. But I was paid even more to warn you!" he said.

"Who paid you to kill me?" she asked.

"Who is the highest authority to suspend you? To put you down and out of your job? To disband the LSS?" he asked, hinting her.

Prakash...

"Don't say his name here. It's not safe!" he said.

"Yeah, no kidding. Assassins can just shoot you easily!" said Radhika, sarcastically.

"Funny..." he said, when he didn't consider it to be amusing at all.

"My dad sent you?" she asked.

"Yeah, now he will let you stay off grid for the rest of your school years! Agent Chopra, you too. That person paid a visit so your dad is afraid. I was going to leave after telling you but it looks like I can't move much!" he said.

She called up someone who arrived in five minutes with a first aid kit.

"You'll help me?" he asked.

"She's a trusted nurse from the school infirmary. After she's done, take this and go as far away from here as possible. My dad may be in danger, as you said. Tell your boss I'm dead. I'll lay low. But we will catch him soon!" She said, handing him a key of a bike.

"Prison won't hold him. You know that! But even still to him, you are dead! Don't worry, he doesn't know how you look! I was going to go! Thanks for understanding." he said.

"Don't mention it..." said Simran.

"I should warn you, though. If you are able to check on the news, then there are serial murders of agents. Do not tell this but I'm part of a team of highly skilled hit men who were paid to kill many of you. So be careful." He said.

"What's your name?" asked Simran.

"Aroop...that's all you get. I'll go in a while, I've got a lot of work to do. So I'll see you soon." He said.

"Will do! Bye!" she said and left with Radhika.

As they go downstairs,

"This is getting very dangerous." Said Radhika.

"So this is what he plans to do with the top 400. Wipe us out. And he'll start with the weakest." Said Simran.

They go to Simran's hostel room and surf on the web for information.

"Oh my god!" they exclaimed.

There were news reports of various murders in schools which were having LOCKERs in them. Simultaneously, they were checking the list of the top 400 too.

"LOCKER 07...Agent Emmanuel...top 400. LOCKER 10, Agent Sharma...top 400. LOCKER 15, Agent Reddy. LOCKER 23, Agent Ray. They are also top 400. This is bad. Very bad." Said Simran.

"He's getting us knocked down like dominoes. We might be next!" said Radhika.

"I'll talk to Princi tomorrow." Said Simran.

In the evening, Natasha leaves and goes to the boys hostel, secretly. Nikhil was packing his bag with a few gadgets. After that, he comes out of his room and was going towards his bike when he caught a glimpse of Natasha, who was sneaking inside when she had heard sounds from both side of the corridor in which she was in.

What is she Doing here?!

Just when they were coming, Nikhil leaps on a rod then he grabs Natasha and pulls her up by her waist which was till the ceiling. They both were pressed against the ceiling.

She looks at him and was about to say something when he immediately closed her mouth.

Down there in a minute two boys of class 10 passed from both sides of the corridor. After the boys leave and were out of sight, they both jump down.

They hear noises of other boys in the corridor before they could talk to each other so Nikhil grabbed her hand and they both sneak out then they make their way towards the parking and stopped in front of Nikhil's bike.

"I have a reputation!" he said.

"I know!" – sees the bag pack – "So do I!" she said.

"What are you Doing here?"

"Where are you going?"

"It's none of your concern and it doesn't explain why you're here!"

"I…uh…wanted to…uh…talk!"

"What!"

"Yeah!"

"You caught me at a bad time so I'll see you tomorrow!"

"Where are you going?"

"Work! And I have to go now!" he said, while getting on his bike.

"What work? And where are you going?" she asked.

"I have to do something dangerous! I need to see a trio of accomplices for Arjun! So bye!"

"Where?"

"The nearby town!"

"But I need to talk to you!"

"Natasha wants to talk to me?"

"What's wrong in it?"

"Nothing! I have to go!"

"Then I'll come too!"

"Why?"

"I think you'll need my help!"

"You'll feel cold on the bike!"

"You won't even be able to talk to them without me!"

"Fine!" – he takes out his jacket – "Here! It really is cold!" said Nikhil.

"Thanks!" said Natasha, while putting it on.

He hands over a helmet and the both put theirs on then she gets onto the bike and puts her hands on his shoulders then the ride off out the gate.

They go on the Rohtang pass and after 20 kilometres on the pass they reach the nearby town in which there is a train station where the students are picked up.

They reach a coffee shop and park their bike. Nearby there was an abandoned looking area. They went into a dark lane just opposite to it in which there was an orange street light in a very dim light.

"Hmm…" said Nikhil, while thinking.

"Oh!" said Natasha when she heard a window break and in a reflex she grabbed his hand.

Nikhil noticed it.

"Let's see…" – giving a fake cough – "Natasha is afraid or she likes to hold my hand!" he said and she immediately removes it.

"D, do you know where we're going?" she asked.

"Of course I do! You still don't drink, right?"

"Yeah…I don't"

"I don't either still…" he said.

"Okay…" she said.

The keep on walking and after taking a turn on their right they find a lonely bar. Both of them go inside.

The place had a medium sized T.V(in which there was a cricket match playing), a billiards table and a small jazz band playing for a few people seated at tables near it.

"We used to do this at school before the top 400! Remember? Get a bottle of water. I'll have a chat with them and when I get back don't say anything till I sit down next to you. Ok?" Nikhil whispered.

They were going to this school and a few others who were part of the previous top 400 made them do it.

I remember, smart guy!

"Okay. There are three surveillance cameras. One over the door, one near the band and one behind the bar…" whispered back Natasha.

Natasha goes and sits at the bar. A bartender comes.

Chapter Nineteen – Enquiries with old faces, a threat!

"May I get you something?" asked the bartender.

"A bottled water. Chilled…" said Natasha.

He goes and takes out a refrigerated bottle of water then gives it to her.

Nikhil goes near the tables and sits down at the farthest table from the jazz band. In the same table were three guys, wearing the same clothes. A black suit and tie with a white shirt and a hat.

"Money or information?" asked the guy in the middle.

"You know what I want…" said Nikhil.

"Just checking. A friend of Arjun. The same one, I presume." Said the guy on the left.

"Let's talk now, shall we?" said Nikhil.

"Okay…well, we just stopped business with him a few years ago. They change their hide outs every year." said the guy on the right.

"The CBI found us with arms deals but Arjun then bailed us out. So we do owe him! We can't help much. When we want to buy anything, the guy on the line says a different place near us all the time and a different person goes there with many people with guns and keep the product. We go take it, then place cash only there and leave. Sometimes they steal stuff then and give it as products to us." said the middle one.

"Would he give something with the product. Like a bill?" asked Nikhil.

"Yes he would. Their business card. When we stopped business with them, they saw us as a threat. They do that to all those who stop business with them. Once they tried to bomb our house but we were saved." Said the right one.

"He had a card given to us then…it seems he always gives these to his threats!" said the left one.

He shows the card.

You are going to die…

"Where did you find it?" asked Nikhil.

"In the bombed area!" said the middle one.

"We used to be four…but now we are three." Said the middle one.

"What happened to the other one?" asked Nikhil.

"Call your girlfriend over there. She knows…" said the one on the left.

Natasha noticed Nikhil calling her over there. She leaves her bottle at the bar, went to them and sat down.

"Abhi? Daniel and…Preetam?" asked Natasha.

"Confused here!" said Nikhil.

"That's good!" said Preetam.

"Prakash has an illegal arms and he would sell different artefacts they steal too!" said Abhi.

"Kapoor Enterprise? We know!" said Natasha.

"Yeah! Well, we don't know much more! Anyway, we need to go!" said Daniel.

"Tell her that we're safe and we love her! And that we will see her soon!" said Abhi.

"Of course!" replied Natasha.

The three of them left and went out from the back door of the bar.

"What was that?" asked Nikhil.

"Abhi is Aparna's older brother. The one killed, Raj, used to be in their gang. They've paid their price in jail. Daniel and Preetam are her other cousins too! After school she is supposed to team up with them. They all would open a contract business together!" explained Natasha.

"What type of contract business?" he asked.

"Assassination. Government approved!" she said.

"A private team with income coming from the central government! Cool!" he said.

They go towards their bike, get on and reach the hostels.

"Thanks!" said Natasha.

"What did you want to talk to me about?" asked Nikhil.

"Another time! See you tomorrow!" she said and walked away.

"Bye!" he called after her and she waved without looking back.

The next day, at 7:00 am, everyone boarded a bus and set off out the gates. Within an hour or two they reached a building painted in military green with three floors.

"A defence sector…" said Ajay.

"Nobody can tap this place!" said the Principal.

"How are you so sure?" asked Indira.

"This was established in June 20th, 1987!" replied Ajay.

"By my father and he's handed it over to me…" said the Principal.

"Everybody goes on her orders and they're trustable!" said Ajay.

The bus stopped at the entrance and everyone was escorted by Diana, who also was able to arrive.

"I got some relief. But he extended my hours of work so whatever plan of ours this is, let's hope it'll work, Vijayanti!" said Diana.

Everybody walked on ahead when Simran tugged on the Principal's shoulder and stopped her at the gate while everyone went ahead.

"Yes, Simran? Anything wrong?" she asked.

How do I tell her? Nobody can help me but myself. Yet I should say indirectly!

"Uh, yeah! I just don't know how to tell you!" she said.

"I'll understand in whatever way you tell me! Come on!" she said.

"Prakash ordered hits on top 400 agents. It could be anybody's life on the line. Anybody! Already four were killed." she said.

"Hmm...then we have to finish this quickly. Basically I planned to get him arrested tomorrow, but it may delay and we will have to do it the day after." She said.

"That means it's dangerous tomorrow. What do I do?" Simran asked.

"You know your status. You would catch the guy if the target is you. I want you to keep a watch on everybody through the surveillance as soon as we get back. Skip school today and tomorrow and stay there. Understood?" she said.

"Yes, ma'am!" she said.

On the second floor conference room, the meeting started.

"Has anyone done any research?" asked Ajay.

Nikhil was the first to stand. He told about the information given by them last night but he didn't say that it was the accomplices of Arjun. Instead he told that they were messengers.

"Anybody else?" asked Diana.

"Um…I've brought the file which has his identity test, criminal record and a few newspaper cuttings of his arrest!" said Simran.

"Perfect. Here's the plan!" said the Principal and she explained the plan.

"But it'll take at least a day to convince the board!" said Diana.

"Then we'll execute the plan the day after tomorrow! Understand?" said the Principal.

"Yes, ma'am!" they said.

They go back to school and in break, Arjun talks to Nikhil while sitting on a table.

"You almost had me thinking that you would tell the truth! But thanks!" said Arjun.

"Yeah! Don't worry! I can handle everything alone!" said Nikhil.

"Oh really!" said Arjun, not believing.

"Yeah! I wouldn't lie to you, man!" said Nikhil.

"You just did!" – saw Natasha coming – "Speaking of whom you took last night, there she is!" said Arjun and he left.

Meanwhile, Aparna gets an unknown call.

"Hello?" she answered.

"You think you can escape your past?! You think you'll live with a great future?! You know who your parents were. Your entire family is that! What makes you think you can be free?!" said some manly voice.

"Who are you and what do you want?" she asked.

"I won't tell you who I am! You will get to know that when I kill you in 37 hours! Not even your brothers can save you!

Watch out, Agent Deshpande!" said the voice and cut the call.

"Hello? Hel-"

37 hours? Should I tell...no...it won't be serious!

Natasha comes and sits down in front of him.

"Hi!" she said.

"Hey!" he said.

"Did he?"

"Yes he did!"

"Sorry!"

"It's okay! I anyway, don't like going without you!"

"Oh! So…"

"Yeah! You wanted to talk to me, right?"

"Yeah!"

"So shoot!"

"I can't shoot here! Just meet me in the basketball court at 1:00!" she said and left.

I wonder...is it about that?

At that time, Riya came and sat in front of him.

"Hi!" she said.

"And you are?" he asked.

"I was thinking if you wanted to go out with me sometime!" she said.

"What?" he asked.

"You! Go out with me!" she said.

"You are a nobody!" he said and he was about to walk away when she grabs his hand.

"Wait! Why not? You don't have anybody, right?" she said.

He pulls away his hand and says "First, don't touch me! Next, I do have somebody!" and he left.

It was quarter to one and suddenly Nikhil wakes up.

Oh, I almost slept completely!

He puts on a pair of jeans and a t-shirt then he went down to the court and saw her sitting with a basketball on the ground.

"Oh good! You're here!" he said and sits down next to her.

"You too!" she said.

"You wanted to talk to me! Shoot!"

"I've found out that Prakash, princi and Simran's father were friends and partners."

"Really? That's interesting."

"Yeah! It is...but there is one thing bothering me."

"What?"

"I wonder if her father can get killed. Her family..."

"That shouldn't happen! She must be knowing about this and her father isn't stupid. But do you know if she has any other family members?" he asked.

"I don't know..." she replied.

"I've asked my dad to look into Kapoor Enterprise a few days ago. He only found their official website but nothing else. That website requires an e-mail ID and a password to see the company's deals." He explained.

"So we can't make a fake ID?" she asked.

"No, actually, the problem is that we can't register freely like that. There is something else to do to access the company." He said.

"And you don't know?" she asked.

"I don't." he said, sighing. "Anything else to know?"

"Nope, I'm done talking! I'll see about that tomorrow." she said and left.

Should I ask Simran? No...not required.

Simran was watching everything everywhere from the surveillance room. She had a jacket on and a bottle of water.

Some romantic scene on a night like this. Anybody can kill them right there. I'm too tensed to sleep any more than during duty. I don't know who is the target but I definitely am not the only one! Damn, this Prakash!

Chapter Twenty –
He's caught! She's dead!

The next day, Natasha told Aparna everything from the bike to the bar to the brother thing to now.

"Thanks for telling me that my other brothers are still fine! Thank you! And that's a nice thing you both have going on!" said Aparna.

"I just feel worried about the situation. This is getting dangerous." she said.

"That's for sure!"

There was a pause.

"Could I ask you something?" asked Aparna.

"Yeah?"

"If I die...then what will you do?"

"What do you mean?"

"What are you going to do about it if I'm killed?"

"Don't joke around! You won't get killed at all! It is foolish to think of such things and to talk about it." she said.

"I'm just saying..."

"You don't have to! The situation is not that dangerous!"

"Just answer me, Natasha. What will you do about it if I die?" asked Aparna, seriously.

Natasha turned and stood in front of her.

"If you get killed, then I will go after your killer and I won't stop until I find the guy and kill the guy." Said Natasha, seriously as well.

"Oh..." said Aparna.

Meanwhile, Nikhil was thinking.

This Simran is very mysterious. She doesn't wish to say anything about herself and her family. She tops in the test without the help of others. Her mother passed away...she didn't come today, I could've asked her a few things. She wouldn't even tell me! So annoying!

He got up and goes to the hostels.

Radhika goes to the surveillance room to see Simran sitting there with a jacket, a couple of water bottles and a blanket.

"What is this?" asked Radhika.

Simran explained her everything.

"Should I help?" she asked.

"Yeah, you keep checking online if any more hits were ordered. And Radhika, stay at one place where I can see you!" said Simran.

"You got it!" she said and left.

Meanwhile, the Principal and her assistant talks to the Director's secretary on phone.

"The plan is going to work!" said Diana.

"Really?" asked Ajay.

"The board agreed!" she said.

"So how many members will they send?" asked Ajay.

"All five members!" she said.

"Your charm is awesome! So let the guards stay here! Tomorrow we'll take care of them after Prakash enters my office! Okay?" said the Principal.

"Yes, ma'am!" both of them said.

She called a few officers from the CBI to arrive at the school to arrest him.

In the evening, Nikhil calls Natasha by using his phone.

"Hello?" answered Natasha.

"Hey! I have to go there again!" said Nikhil.

"Yeah! So?" she asked.

"So come on!" he said.

"Why?" she asked.

"Please? Just come down! I'm waiting on my bike!" he said.

"Fine!" she said and he cut the phone.

She comes down and sees him on his bike waiting for her.

She gets on without a word and they go to the nearby town again.

Simran sees them going.

Damn them! No, don't go! It's a Sunday! Stay! It's 1:30!
Dammit!

Arjun just then came for duty.

"Thank goodness you came! Stay on duty! I will be right back! Bye!" she said left while putting on her jacket.

"What the-" he started.

"Just watch everybody!" she said and left.

She got on the hover board she fixed with a helmet and sunglasses on then left without anybody knowing to the nearby town and went inside the coffee shop, sat down at a table in a corner near the window with a menu card before they came in. They came in and sat down at a table in another corner on the same side in the coffee shop.

"What are we Doing here?" asked Natasha.

"Now I have to talk!" he said.

"You brought me out here to talk?! When it's not safe?"

"Yeah, I did!"

"Fine, go ahead!"

"As far as I know, Prakash was arrested by his own partners."

"No, not really! They didn't do much. But they met him later and scolded him. He retorted back at them and they stopped talking."

"I didn't know that. You sure?"

"Yeah, I know." she said.

"Hmm..." he said.

"So, anything else?" she said.

"Anything on Simran?" he asked.

"No…she is so confusing. I can't find out anything about her. She must've hidden all of her information through her hacking. Same with Radhika. This is so annoying!" she said.

"Yeah, tell me about it. She thinks that she can be better than us just because she topped. I understand her winning, but everybody is taking a special liking to her, especially Princi." Said Nikhil.

"Yeah…she wasn't punished at all. And whenever Princi sees me, I feel as if she knows about the training we've received before." Said Natasha.

"If that was so, why make me an in-charge? It's okay…we'll see about her at some other time." He said.

"Hmm…good. Anything else?" she asked.

"Nope. You want to know anything?" he asked.

"You won't tell the truth if I ask!" said Natasha.

"Well, just the one I wanted to see." said Riya, just arriving with a few others sitting down at a table while she came to theirs.

"Where did you come from?" asked Natasha.

"Oh yeah! You should go because I have to talk to him!" she said, while pointing.

"Great, not you again! Just" Nikhil started but Natasha said "Shut up" and she got up.

"You must be new here! You are in class 10. I'm in class 11. I'm also his ex so I will definitely not go! " she said, while grabbing her arm by her wrist and started to twist it.

"Ah! Leave my hand! Ah! Fine! Ah!" she cried in pain.

"Fine what?" asked Natasha.

"I'll go I'll go I'll go! Ah!" she cried out and she left her hand then she went away.

Whoa, she's pissed off!

She came back and sat down.

"Why was she here?" she asked.

"She's bothering me! First Raghav, then Arjun!" he said.

"Stay away from her." she said.

"I know, I'm trying." he said.

"Okay..."

"Nat, you really can ask me. I promise I'll answer truthfully."

"Sure?"

"I know you've been meaning to ask."

"Really?"

"Yeah! So ask me." he said.

"When are you going to forgive me and forget what had happened?" she said.

"Depends. You still haven't learned to control your attitude. I'm afraid to say anything about this until you control it."

"You always speak in riddles anyway. Even if you forgive me you still won't directly say it! It's annoying."

"You want me back or not?"

"Yeah! I do. I will be better. I just need to adjust."

"Fine, I'll take your word for it."

"Just give a direct answer next time."

"Fine, then when the time comes, I will say that I forgive you." he said, while getting up.

"Okay." she said.

They got up and left after paying. Simran was watching everything.

Seriously, at a time like this they have to do this shit! They can get killed. But they are fine. So far so good...

A waitress comes to her.

"Excuse me, you didn't order anything else except that water bottle." She said.

"Some people come here and don't order anything! Here!" – giving money for the bottle – "I'll buy something real next time!" said Simran and left after seeing Nikhil and Natasha leave.

They get on and go back to school with Simran trailing after them. Radhika calls her.

"Yeah, any update?" asked Simran.

"At LOCKER 19, Agent Srinivas of the top 400 died a couple hours ago." Said Radhika.

"Damn..." said Simran.

"We can't do anything, can we?" said Radhika.

"If we try sending warnings, they will come for us before we are even ready! I'm sorry but we cannot do anything!" said Simran.

"Okay, see you soon. I'll check the others at the hostels." Said Radhika and cut the call.

Aparna was in her room thinking about that call when her phone rings again.

"Hello?" she asked.

"I hope you've spent your last day wisely! Tomorrow you will be killed at the time when nobody is there!" said that voice.

"No way! Don't you threaten me!" she shouted but he cut the call.

Is this really going to happen?! No way!

Simran goes back to the Surveillance and Arjun was still there. She went inside and shut the door.

"Where were you? Did you sleep?" he asked.

"Yeah, I did!" she said.

The next day, in the early morning, everyone meet the Principal in the school grounds.

"Where are all of the students?" asked Ajay.

"They have been sent for trekking and will be back by tomorrow with the teachers. All right?" said the Principal.

"Yes, ma'am!" everyone said

They discussed the plan again and then left. Simran informs the Principal.

"Good job. Now everybody is alert. You may go and be ready! Let's do this!" she said.

"Yes, ma'am!" she said.

"Be careful with yourself!" said the Principal.

"I got it." Said Simran and left while loading a gun and putting it in her jacket.

Looks like I'll have to use this now...

They waited for the Director to arrive. After an hour he did and the Principal took him into the building.

As soon as he went inside, everyone sneaked up to the gates and towards the guards. At all of the gates they ambushed and killed the guards then the agents stood there.

"Nikhil coming in! North gate secure!" said Nikhil on his talkie.

"Radhika coming in! East gate secure!" said Radhika on her talkie.

"Aakash from the West gate! It's secure!" he said on his talkie.

"Gaurav coming in! South gate secure!" he said.

"Good! Stay put for more!" said Nikhil on his talkie.

"Simran reporting from the Surveillance! Open the North gate. He's here!" said Simran on her talkie.

"There's a slight problem, Agent Khanna! Agent Patel, he has a lot of reinforcements with him asking for entry here!" said Gaurav on his talkie.

"Give the number!" said Arjun.

"I'm not sure!" said Gaurav.

"Guys, Shreya here at the hostel terrace! I can see the four gates clearly!" said Shreya through her talkie. "It doesn't look good!"

"Elaborate on that!" said Simran.

"Neerav from the school terrace! There are reinforcements at all gates and they are requesting permission to enter! You better decide fast!" said Neerav talking through his talkie with binoculars.

"Grant them entry! Agent Rao's orders!" said Ajay on his talkie.

How the-fine!

"Nikhil! Indira! Request permission!" everyone at the gates said.

"Oh no!!" cried out Natasha when she reached the school ground.

Aparna was shot dead in the chest twice by one of Prakash's agents. She immediately chased after that agent and elbowed him down. She tied him up to a chair.

"Natasha! Do you know where is Aparna?" asked Rishi on his talkie.

"Rishi. Listen to me carefully. Get to the ground and drag the body into one of the classrooms. Now! We will have a lot of gun fight any minute!" she said.

"I don't understand!" he said as he ran from the south gate.

"Aparna's shot dead. Don't break down now! Get her out of there! I caught her killer!" shouted Natasha.

Rishi had reached the ground and froze on seeing her. He immediately picked her up and carried her into a classroom and shut the doors.

"Nikhil. Do not call me now. I'm held up a bit! So is Rishi. Do not come yet to find us. Just fix this crap first! Okay? Do not call Aparna either!" said Natasha on her talkie.

"Nat, what happened? What's wrong?" asked Nikhil.

"Just do what I say!!" ordered Natasha.

"Indira, give the decision! Now!" said Nikhil.

"Authorised. Entry to the vehicles!" said Indira.

They opened the gates and the vehicles immediately came in. Prakash got down and went to the Principal's cabin.

In the Principal's office, the Director was seated with the Principal accompanied with a few other agents of his.

"So Vijayanti…what am I going to do with you?" he asked.

"You know, I think your other face was better before the plastic surgery. You looked more… recognizable!" she replied.

"I'll put you in the file room…and if you're lucky enough then I might fire you!" he said.

"You can't do that, Prakash!" she replied.

"Yes, I can!" he said.

"What are you really here for?" she asked.

"I'm implementing a new policy which I made. I'm rounding up all the LOCKERs around the country! And I'm going to give the top 400 a new job as my personal agent team!" said the Director.

"Top 400 or top 50? You are killing them one by one!" she shouted.

"No you can't!" said a board member from behind him.

"Sir!" – he gets up and salutes – "How did?" he started but another member interrupted.

"You are under arrest for disguising as a candidate in the elections and you have the right to remain silent." he said.

"Nope! You can't because I have others to do so!" said the Director and clapped once.

Immediately, agents of his came and grabbed all of them and dragged them outside. He immediately sent a few to the basement to fetch the LOCKER articles. The agents immediately left to the basement but they were shot on point blank.

"Agent Murthy here with Agent Bhattacharya, Pandey and Desai. Targets shot! Begin attack now before he notices some agents missing!" said Aneesh through his talkie.

"Arjun, contact the base! Send a signal for troops! There are way too many agents here!" said Nikhil.

"Already done! They are coming in a few minutes! Let's go!" said Arjun.

Everybody immediately left for the ground and attacked the agents! Vijayanti elbowed the agent holding her down and punched him unconscious. She also grabs a gun and shoots the agents holding the board members. The Director went into his car but was pulled out by Ajay. Prakash punched Ajay and they started fighting. But suddenly, Simran grabbed a gun to aim it at an agent clutching Arjun by the neck with another gun pointed at his head.

"You can't shoot, Simran!" shouted Arjun.

"That's right! I can shoot him a lot faster than you!" said the agent.

She didn't lower her gun.

"Put it down, Khanna! Your friend has a point!" said the agent.

She still pointed at his head.

"Simran, don't! Don't do it!" cried out Arjun.

"Arjun!" said Simran.

"What? Please don't shoot! You won't be able to!" said Arjun.

"Simran, do it!" shouted Radhika from a distance when she stopped.

"Arjun, don't tell anybody!" she said.

"Don't tell what?" he asked.

She suddenly shot the agent's hand in which the gun was pointed and he let go of Arjun who ran and as the agent pointed again Simran shot a bullet on his head and he fell back dead.

"That! You could shoot that?! How can you do that?! That was so quick and-" Arjun reacted so frantically that he fainted.

"You did great! You still don't want to shoot anybody?" asked Radhika, while standing outside the infirmary with Simran as Arjun was lying down on a bed.

"I can't! I can't do it!" said Simran.

"But you are the best. You've learnt from the best!" said Radhika.

"That person who taught me is the best but I've learnt to stay out of trouble through keeping us hidden!" she said.

"I beg of you, Simran! He will find you one day! The one you are hiding from! I want you to promise me that you will brush up in shooting since you are already starting to hack again!" said Radhika.

"I promise, I'll train later in the holidays! I might as well do it. But nobody should know!" said Simran, sighing.

"Nobody will!" said Radhika.

The nurse came out.

"He was just shocked. He's just unconscious and he's sleeping right now! It's normal, whenever this type of situation occurs he faints. I have to go so one of you keep an eye on him!" she said.

"Thank you!" said Simran and the nurse left.

Simran went inside and sat down next to Arjun on a chair while he slept. Radhika went to see the others. In a few minutes, Arjun opened his eyes and looked around. He found Simran dabbling on her phone and nobody else.

"Ow..." he groaned as he tried to get up.

He sat up straight with his back on his pillow.

"Well, that was quick. I never thought you would be on the bed with IV fluids going in you." Said Simran, without looking up.

"Oh, shit. Not you. Anybody but you!" Arjun said, feeling weak.

"Yup...sucks huh. I told you so!" She said.

"I'm already in a pathetic condition. Don't make it worse." He groaned.

"Oh, look who's talking now. I'm just enjoying which I don't usually do." She said.

"Yes, I know. Your life is depressing. So is mine." He said.

"Do you remember anything on how you were saved?" asked Simran, looking up at him.

"How did you save me?" he asked, looking at her by tilting his head a bit.

"Another time." She said.

"That means never, right?" he said.

"Yup. So this is your health issue, huh. Makes sense." She said.

"It's...damn...don't tell anyone...please...don't!" He said, weakly.

"Whatever. And yeah, when you are ready to get up, then we should go to class 4." Said Simran.

"I feel weak. I can't." he said.

"Well, well, well, mr. tough guy! Surprising decision!" she said, got up and went towards the door.

"And yeah, next time you see me like this, then pretend to care at least." He said.

"Let's see…" she said and left.

Meanwhile, Natasha was in the storeroom with the tied agent.

"I've had enough of you!" she shouted after beating him up.

"You can't get anything out of me!" said the agent.

"Oh really!" she said.

She beat him up twice and thrice really hard.

"Okay! okay! It was Prakash!" he cried out.

"I'm not satisfied!" she yelled.

She continued to beat him up.

Just then the army from the research base arrived and saved the day. Within minutes, the Director was captured and taken away by the army.

They shoved him inside a car and drove away.

The agents were called and they lined up.

"Since you were the runner up in the elections, Agent Vijayanti Rao is here-by appointed as the Director of the LSS branch of the IB! You will have a desk at the IB HQ and I request you to find your replacement for the LSS recruitment committee chairperson and the in charge of LOCKER 01." Announced another board member.

"Yes, sir!" she said.

After the board left, Nikhil contacted Rishi.

"Everybody get to class 4! Now!" said Rishi.

They immediately went and got a huge shock at seeing Aparna's body with Rishi crying and the nurse with her head down.

"Oh god...how did this happen?!" asked the Director (Vijayanti Rao).

Simran was shocked the most.

Oh no...how the hell could I let this happen! I couldn't save her! Dammit! Damn that Prakash! I have to speak to Vijayanti ma'am!

Rishi told everything as he let down a few tears. Neerav went and hugged Rishi and he cried more. Nikhil immediately left to look for Natasha.

"Okay fine!! Enough!! I'll tell! Stop!" cried out the agent.

"Tell me why he ordered it!! Now!!" she yelled.

"Her parents were in his business! They were talking and she had heard them. Her parents told her everything when she confronted them! But she didn't shut up! She was only 7. She thought that she was in jail but it was actually an old dungeon of ours. She told her brother when she went to see him in jail. We killed him. Then we got an inside job done. Prakash and her father sent that letter to suspend her. I can't tell anymore now!" he said.

"You're worth nothing to Prakash. You will be killed by him the minute I let you go! Tell me everything! Now!!" she shouted.

"Some bitch cleared her name. But we couldn't leave it at that!" said the agent.

"So you killed her..." she said.

"After warning her! That's it!" he said.

She sat down on her chair and her eyes were red. Just then, Nikhil arrived.

"Natasha, I was looking for you! Did he tell stuff?" asked Nikhil.

"Yeah..." she said.

Just then more agents arrived to help clean up the mess. Two of them took Aparna's body and Natasha handed over the killer to the head agent and they left.

Meanwhile, Simran and Neerav were talking. Shreya noticed from a distance.

"I don't know what to do! Rishi just...he's dead inside!" said Neerav.

"I know. I think you two should go somewhere. He liked her. He has to get past that!" she said.

"Yeah...how do you know so much on this?" he asked.

"My mom? Bye!" said Simran and left.

Just then, Shreya comes.

"Hey. Is Rishi okay?" she asked.

"No..." he said.

"Natasha got everything out of the killer. She'll tell us later on what happened. Come on!" she said.

"Where?" he asked.

"We'll take a walk. You need it!" she said.

"You don't have to worry about me!" he said.

"I'm your girlfriend! I should worry!" she said.

"Yeah you are! But lately, you weren't that!"

"What makes you think so?"

"You think Simran has something going on with me!"

"A bit, yeah!"

"Well, I'm just helping her annoy Arjun." he asked.

"Okay. Well, come on!" said Shreya.

They go for a walk.

After that, Arjun stops Simran.

"Didn't you say you felt weak?" she asked.

"I'm fine!" he said.

"Good!" she said and turned to leave but stopped.

"Miss know it all! How did you shoot him?" asked Arjun.

"I don't shoot. Okay, well. I think you heard the news!" she said.

"Don't think I'm underestimating you again but are you okay?" he replied.

"Yeah. You want something?"

"I just want us to be proper partners because we need to work together!"

"Nikhil lectured you?"

"Yeah, why?"

"You will never agree to say this otherwise! You are a jerk!"

"Would you stop that?! I've actually given this thing that we have a chance when we spent the night in the meeting room!"

"What chance? We were forced to!"

"I had a weapon! I could've escaped from the window but I didn't!" he said.

"No, I just hate you! That will never change!" she said.

"Same here!" he said.

"And you had a knife? Expect me to believe that?" she said.

"It's a fact!" he said.

"No, here is one: If you screw up like that night again, we all will kill you!" she replied and left.

The night continued and they all were in their hostels and everything was back to normal...or was it?

Chapter Twenty One –
It's not over yet!

Everything functioned as usual but everybody still was sad for Aparna. It was still depressing. But after Prakash getting arrested, the murders were stopped. The top 400 was saved. Most of them.

In the second last week of school, one day, the DIRECTOR had her bags packed and took a last look at the school. Everyone arrived to see her off. At that time, a vehicle arrived at the North gate. From it stepped out a woman resembling a bit of Vijayanti whom she went and hugged.

"My sister, who used to be in RAW. Agent Rao! She'll be your Principal now!" announced the Director.

"I've got everything taken care of!" said the new Principal.

The Director left after the good byes and everyone heads back to the hostels.

On another day, which was the last exam in the first term, in the examination hall, before going in, Arjun stopped Simran.

"Listen!" – he grabbed her and pulled her away from the hall around a wall for a while – "First, are you Doing good?" he asked.

Asking me how I'm Doing?

"Of course, I am!" she replied.

"Well, in case you haven't noticed, I'm not Doing too well! My head is not in the right space because of Aparna and your confusing me and not telling how you saved me!" he said.

"You don't need to know!" she said.

"I still feel weak...this hasn't happened before. This problem didn't affect so much on me before! I am not able to do anything right now! So tell me how it happened!" he said.

"No, it's not necessary!" she said.

"Stop making me need you. I can't take your help anymore!" he said.

"So what if I help? I do it out of interest! You don't have to owe me anything!" she said.

"Come on! Tell me!" he said.

"I will not!" she said.

"Please!" he said.

"It's none of your business!" she said and left.

After the exam, every girl assembled in the meeting room while the boys went to their hostel rooms. In the boys hostel room of Neerav and Arjun, they both and the rest of the boys were also there.

"A letter?" asked Arjun.

"Ma'am is really old school!" said Nikhil.

"Amateur…" said Siddharth.

"Like your girlfriend?" asked Raghav.

"Shut up, man." He said.

"I'll read it out!" said Arjun.

There are many reasons on which these things could not be spoken to you all about. I have received information regarding: Other people, who are trying to control the system, have bad intentions just like Prakash. Since you all are part of the top 400 agents of the IB, you will definitely be a target. On the other hand though, I'm going to have to fix everything in the agency which may ruin it. So don't feel offended if I arrive for regular checks. But you will be receiving missions after your exams. Till then, stay safe. They may also want to recruit you. Aparna's father was murdered. Her mother disappeared. Prakash is still in jail.

I'll be on conference anytime. You may just use the link in the meeting room. Take care of the LOCKER. Oh, burn after reading.

Vijayanti Rao, DIRECTOR

"Recruit us?" asked Neerav.

"She said that we need not worry!" said Aneesh.

"But still…" said Aakash.

"Prakash won't be there for long, you know." said Arjun.

"He's right. What if that crazy mafia boss comes for you again, Arjun?" asked Raghav.

"Are you crazy?! No! We've taught them a good lesson." said Neerav.

"Yeah when we were not supposed to. Who had a knife when they brutally injured three guys?" said Nikhil.

"What's it to you?" asked Gaurav.

"Oh, so you did it!" he said.

"Don't be crazy!" said Gaurav.

"But you know who did!" said Aakash.

"I'm not saying anything!" said Gaurav.

"Actually, those three were not fit for interrogation due to all of those wounds. They are still in a hospital with strict bed rest and security." Said Nikhil.

"What a shame…" said Siddharth.

"And Arjun, remember. I won't tolerate what you did that time." Said Nikhil. Arjun looked away while rolling his eyes.

"Hmm…" said Gaurav, while thinking.

Simran, what did you do?

Meanwhile, all of the girls chat with the Director in the meeting room and the Director tells them about the letter to the boys.

"That's it?" asked Natasha.

"Afraid so. Boys don't need to know everything." Said the Director.

"So is it over?" said Simran.

"I don't know but it's not surprising when you ask. He has many accomplices and partners. All of them are corrupt, no doubt. Not just here but he has a few CIA, Russian, Chinese and MI6 agents as well. He has connections with terrorist groups too." Explained the Director.

"So he ordered hits on us..." Said Shreya, realising.

"So I'm going to show you a few pictures, all right? These are people associated with Prakash and his company. Very soon they may arrive in India to carry out their arms deals since we took out most of their associates." said the Director.

"Yes ma'am." The rest said.

The first picture displays. It showed an American type of man in his 30s with curly hair, whitish skin and a tattoo of some design on his neck.

"I've seen him!" said Aanya.

"So did I!" said Ankita.

"But I don't remember where!" said Radhika.

"Brad…at the CIA, he was known as O. Arjun's boss, remember? One of FBI's most wanted! He got out already?" said Simran, remembering.

"Even I didn't know that! Where's the source?" asked the Director.

"PC number 02763, database 04 in the Tihar jail records!" said Simran.

"No showing off about that to anybody! He got out three days after the elections. I didn't know that he was with Prakash." replied the Director.

Another picture showed. It was a thin, whitish man with smooth brown hair. He looked 25 and short.

"What about him?" asked Indira.

"Dean Robin. MI6, double agent, on the run, good with calculations." Said the Director.

Another picture showed but it was a picture of a girl this time. She looked Chinese, in her 30s with long straight black hair on whitish skin. She was a bit tall.

"And her?" asked Priya.

"Lu, Chinese, I don't know her last name but she is known by that, also a double agent and she designs and she makes her own weapons from bombs to guns." Replied the Director, while explaining.

Another picture of a girl is shown. She was Indian, in her 20s, with curly black hair and tanned skin.

"Next! She's well known!" said the Director.

"Who?" the rest of them asked.

"Niharika Rai. Ex-CBI, robbed LOCKER 9, done some murders, double agent and my sister!" said Natasha.

"Oh…we're" they started but she cut them off.

"I can so live with it!" said Natasha.

Another picture was shown and it was a guy. At seeing it Shreya was wide-eyed. He looked Indian and young, at least 18. He's a bit fair with black styled hair and normal height.

"Maybe you can enlighten us, Agent Fernandez…" said the Director.

"Robbed the entire LOCKER 11, assassin, double agent, con man, Rohit. Sorry but he never told me his last name whenever we met." She said.

"Oh!" the rest said.

"What?" Simran was surprised.

After the meeting, Simran started to interrogate Shreya in their hostel room.

"Was he your ex-boyfriend you told me about?" she asked.

"Long time ago! I was stupid! Can we not?" asked Shreya.

"No wonder you're so protective of yourself! Can't even trust me and you start questioning Neerav!"

"Simran, I trust you and I even trust Neerav! I asked just like that!"

"He at least won't do anything like that! He was helping me! That's it!"

"He tells me everything!"

"Oh, so he knows. What about your parents?"

"Well, about that thing, my parents don't know. Never did and I don't plan on telling them!"

"You don't have to!"

"What about you?"

"What about me? I got no issues!"

"The way I hear you on the phone with your dad…you have issues. Family ones!"

"You ever experienced the feeling where someone is trying to kill you, but you can't kill that person?"

"No…what happened?"

"Some other time, Shreya! I'll tell you if you tell me!"

"Okay! And yeah, I and Neerav are together! So don't get ideas!" said Shreya.

"I won't! From when?" asked Simran.

"At the IB Kolkata training camp!" said Shreya.

The next morning, Simran went to the meeting room, locked the door and opened the laptop then connected to the Director.

"Hello, Simran! You wished to speak to me?" asked the Director.

"Ma'am, I'm sorry! I didn't know! I swear, I did check her! She was alive, she really was and-" Simran started apologising.

"Stop Simran! It's not your fault! Your work was done! It seems Aparna was getting calls of threats from the past two days. She didn't tell anybody and she didn't take it seriously. That was her fault!" said the Director.

"Okay..." she said.

"I trust you, Simran. Do not ask me why, I just do. And I trust you to keep everybody under control. Close people to Aparna would want to dig deeper and disturb our investigations. Make sure that doesn't happen." She said.

"Yes, ma'am." Said Simran.

"But it's difficult. She was hit by a professional. So our intelligence may close the case. Also her relatives want her body quickly. You know how religious they are." She explained.

"Understood." She said.

"That associate of Arjun...how do you know?" she asked.

"He...told me. That's the guy who led the attempted robbery here." She said.

"Seriously? Damn...I'll have to go see that. Make sure that your partner doesn't go calling or meeting his old friends." She said.

"Got it!" she said.

"Anything else?" she asked.

"He'll escape, won't he?" she said.

"It's possible! But we'll be ready! One more thing! I want you to come to Delhi and meet me privately! Okay?" she said.

"All right but why?" asked Simran.

"It's for something very important! I can only get you to do it. So definitely come!" said the Director.

Later on, everyone, who were going home, were being seen off at the station. On one train, Indira was about to enter when Aakash stops her.

"Indu!" he said.

"Yes, Aakash!" said Indira.

He immediately gave a quick hug and pulled away.

"What was that for?" she asked.

"Just for the moment. I still don't like you! Bye!" he said, winked and left.

Asshole...

Simran speaks to Gaurav while helping him take his bags to the station platform.

"Nikhil and Natasha may prove to be trouble later to you. I've heard her get scolded by the new Agent Rao for what she did to the suspect." He said.

"It was nothing. He's totally fine." She said.

"Yeah he was. Not near to the guys almost killed last time." He said, looking at her. She sighed.

"You knew, huh." She said.

"Just me, though. Everyone thought it was me. Just be careful next time." He said.

"I can handle it." She said.

"Do you usually get violent?" he asked.

"No, I rarely do. You don't have to know about these things. Trust me, I won't kill." She said.

"That's all I needed to know." He said.

Priya gives a good bye to Ankita.

"I guess, I was wrong about you!" said Priya.

"I guess, I was wrong about you too! So call me!" said Ankita.

"Will do!" said Priya.

Radhika bids adieu to Gaurav.

"So, I guess I'll see you in a week!" he said.

"Sure! I'll be here, I guess!" she said.

"Okay! You are the first understanding girl whom I've met!" he said.

"Thanks. You are the first normal guy whom I've met!" she said.

"Thank you!" he said, while grabbing his bags and getting on the train.

"Agent Oberoi? I mean, Gaurav!" she called out.

"Yeah?" he asked.

"When you come back, you'd better not be disturbed again. Or else you will have to tell me!" she said.

"Okay!" he said.

In a few minutes his train left and she went up the over bridge. Simran was there.

"Hey!" she said.

"Hey..." she said.

"The new Director called me to Delhi. I'll go and come back tomorrow." she said.

"Hmm...don't worry, I'll drop you anywhere and pick you up too." she said.

"Thanks. And could you just find a place for practice?" she asked.

"Sure, you teach me too." she said.

"Okay..." said Simran.

Arjun goes up the platform bridge after seeing Nikhil go. They had one brief eye contact and Nikhil left. The trains left from the station. The first term ended giving ten days for the Dussera vacation.

Until next time...

Printed in the United States
By Bookmasters